Step-Chain

All over the country children go to stay with step-parents, stepbrothers and stepsisters at the weekends. It's just like an endless chain. A step-chain. *You Can't Fancy Your Stepsister* is the second link in this step-chain.

I'm Ollie. My parents split up a while ago, and my brother and I live with Mum and Peter, my stepdad. He's more laid back than my real dad, so going on a holiday with him should be fun. Except that Peter's daughters are coming along, too. Girls! I just know there'll be trouble . . .

Collect the links in the step-chain! You never know who you'll meet on the way...

Step-Chain

YOU CAN'T FANCY YOUR STEP-SISTER

Ann Bryant

Mammoth

For my special friend, Val

First published in Great Britain 2001
by Mammoth
an imprint of Egmont Children's Books Limited
a division of Egmont Holding Limited
239 Kensington High Street
London W8 6SA

Series editor: Anne Finnis

ISBN 0 7497 4323 9

1 3 5 7 9 10 8 6 4 2

Typeset by Avon Dataset Ltd, Bidford on Avon, B50 4JH
(www.avondataset.co.uk)
Printed and bound in Great Britain by
Cox & Wyman Ltd, Reading, Berkshire

CONTENTS

Step-Chain

Robert Dale
Amanda Cranshaw

Charlie(12)
Frankie(13)

Steve Fowler

Debra Dale

Sarah(12)
Mark(10)
Clemmie(6)

Liz Fowler

Paul(12)
Jack(16)

Simon Jones
Tigs Jones

Susannah(10)
Rachel(12)

Tony Simpson
Caroline Simpson

Craig(15)
Hannah(13)

Alison Rutherford

Sean McPherson

Read on to discover all the links . . .

1 THE COUNTDOWN

My name's Oliver Banks. That's the longest version, strictly reserved for teachers – '*Oliver Banks, I don't appear to have received your home-work.*' Then there's Oliver, which is what Mum calls me when she's not happy. But my friends all call me Ollie.

I live with my mum and my stepdad, Peter. He's really cool. He jokes around a lot and isn't as strict as my real dad. Not that I like my real dad any less than Peter. It's just that he's not so laid back.

Right now it's the summer holidays and I'm counting down the days till we go away for a fortnight's holiday to Devon. Only three to go. I *think* I'm looking forward to it, but I'm not totally sure. The people going from my family are me, my mum, Peter and my brother Rory.

Fine so far. But . . . get this! Peter wants to bring his two daughters along. They don't live with us. They live with their mum, but come here to visit their dad (Peter) quite often. They're called Frankie and Charlie. I'm usually at my dad's when they come here, so I don't really get to see them all that much. Once or twice Charlie's been here on her own, and she seems OK, mucking about with Rory in the garden or on his precious computer.

But going on holiday together – that's different. I bet Frankie and Charlie don't want to go away with two boys, any more than I want to go away with two girls.

'Oliver?'

Uh-oh! Mum didn't sound too happy.

'Yeah?' I answered, opening my bedroom door.

'How many times have I got to tell you to take your trainers off at the back door?' she called up the stairs.

'But I came in at the front. With Peter.'

'I realise that. There's a trail of muddy footprints going through the hall and all the way upstairs. I presume they go right into your bedroom. Come to the top of the stairs. Let me look at you.'

I quickly took the trainers off without undoing the laces, then went to the top of the stairs.

'Oh, Ollie. What *am* I going to do with you?'

'What's wrong? I've taken my trainers off.'

'But your tracksuit bottoms and your shirt are absolutely filthy! Do your friends go home looking as though they've been having a mud bath?'

Mum was exaggerating and she knew it. 'You can't help getting dirty if you're playing football, Mum. Peter didn't tell me off,' I couldn't resist adding.

'Peter probably didn't even notice. Anyway, I'm not arguing about it. Go and have a bath and by the time you've done that, dinner will be ready.'

And that was when I remembered that I was supposed to be taking a video back to Sam Cotteril's. I'd promised I'd definitely do it today, because it belongs to his much older brother, who's going ape because I keep forgetting to give it back.

The trouble was, knowing Mum, there was no chance she'd let me go round to Sam's even if I got down on my bended knee and begged. So there was only one thing for it.

I ran the bath water at top force, then turned the taps off, shut the bathroom door, and sneaked downstairs and out the front door with the video. I got to Sam's in a record seven minutes.

'Hiya, Ollie. You look puffed,' he said, opening the door. 'You can't be very fit. You ought to get yourself in training.'

He grinned because everyone knows that Sam is the least fit person in the universe.

'Cut out the chat, Sam. I'm supposed to be in the bath. I'm risking another big blow-up from Mum, bringing this back for you.'

'Bet you'd like to have a quick go on my new computer game though,' he said, grinning even more and opening the door wider. 'It only takes a few minutes and it's demon, I can tell you.'

I knew I should have just said no. Sam must have seen the hesitation on my face. (He could hardly have missed it – I was biting my lip and screwing my eyes up trying not to give in to temptation.)

'The thing is, Ollie,' said Sam, yanking me in through the front door, 'if you go home straight away your body won't have had time to recover, but if you just rest for a few minutes you'll get back much faster, honest.'

It seemed to make sense.

'OK. Only a few minutes though.'

Sam's mum called out when Sam and I were practically at the top of the stairs. She's scary, Sam's mum. Her voice sounds too loud for the room. You're not supposed to use the word fat, so let's just say she's quite large and she always wears big swirly dresses, in bright colours like orange. Her hair's weird too. Sort of speckled blondey grey and shiny.

'Is that Oliver Banks, by any chance?' she boomed up the stairs. I turned round and gave her a shaky smile.

'Hello, Mrs Cotteril.' I've never had the guts to call her Pammy, which is what she likes people to call her. It just sounds stupid.

'I'm glad you're here, Oliver, because Samson –' I tried not to smirk – 'tells me that your family is off to North Devon in a few days' time, too. Such a coincidence!'

The bangles on her arm started jangling, like she needed a fanfare to go with her loud voice. I made a noise that was supposed to show that I agreed about the coincidence but didn't really want to talk about it any more.

'Ollie's only got a minute, Mum,' said Sam, going up the last two stairs. I was about to follow when . . .

'Are you going anywhere near Brinton on your travels, by any chance, Oliver?' Mrs C's big voice rang round the stairwell.

'Er . . . I'm not sure –'

'What's the name of the place where you're staying? Hmm?'

'Er . . . Darasham.'

She clapped her hands together and the clap echoed all the way up the stairs.

'Incredible! Such a coincidence! It's scarcely a stone's throw from Brinton. Marvellous news. I shall telephone your mother straight away and arrange a little get-together. We're staying with my sister and her daughter. Samson wasn't too sure that he wanted to spend a week in all-female company, were you, Samson?'

I whacked Sam's leg as subtly as I could to get him to stop his mum from phoning my mum. That would be just brilliant, wouldn't it, when I was supposed to be in the bath? Sam must have thought I was trying to get away so we could play the computer game, because he turned and headed for his bedroom. His mum was still banging on in her foghorn voice, 'But now you know Oliver is going to be around, I think we might detect a bit of an improvement in your attitude, hmm?'

'Er . . . actually, Mrs Cotteril, Mum's out at the moment. I'll tell her to phone you when she gets back.'

'All right, Oliver. Thank you, dear.'

And she went off singing in a high warbly voice in a foreign language. Poor Sam! I was glad my mum was quite an ordinary sort of mother so my friends couldn't take the rip out of me. It'd be good if he was near us on holiday though. But something told me Mum wasn't going to be too pleased. I don't think she's ever liked Mrs Cotteril all that much.

It was beginning to look like coming to Sam's was one big mistake.

2 PETER THE PEACEMAKER

It was twenty-three minutes later when I got home. I'd got a key for the front door but I knew it'd make a noise when I opened it, so I reckoned the back would be safer. The only problem was getting through the kitchen without Mum seeing me. I peered in through the window and saw that the coast was clear. The windows were pretty steamed up though, which meant that dinner must be nearly ready, so Mum would be back in the kitchen at any minute.

The back door hardly made a sound as I opened it. I just had to get upstairs without being seen. I took off my trainers and tiptoed, quiet as a cat burglar, through the kitchen and the hall, then up the stairs. (Rory was in his bedroom. I could hear racing car noises coming from his computer.) I crept into the bathroom, took all my clothes off, sat in the bath for about five seconds, ripped the icicles off me, got straight out again, rubbed myself dry, then went back to my room to find some clean clothes. I couldn't help smiling to myself as I got dressed. It was so easy to fool Mum.

'Shall I put these dirty jeans in the washing machine?' I asked her, trying not to sound *too* much of a creep, as I went into the kitchen a few minutes later.

I could only just make her out in the middle of the steam from all the pans. She was straining the peas. Perfect timing, Ollie!

'Yes, that's what we normally do with dirty clothes,' she replied. I didn't like that sarcastic tone. It meant she was still cross. Dunno why – I'd had a bath (or so she thought) and I'd even brought my jeans down for the wash. 'Put the plates on the table then go and tell Rory and Peter that it's ready, will you?'

The four of us were tucking into this cheesy pasta stuff, when all became clear.

'Frankie phoned,' Rory said.

He had a sort of lopsided grin on his face. This was the expression my sly little brother always wore when he was stirring things – trying to get me into trouble. I'd thought he was talking to Mum, but everyone was staring at me. Uh-oh! About to be sussed, Ollie!

'Yeah?' I said, flashing my innocent look round the table, even though I could see what was coming a mile off.

'She wanted to speak to you,' Mum told

me, raising her eyebrows slightly.

'So . . . did you say I was in the bath?' Keep cool.

'I knocked on the bathroom door to find out how long you were going to be,' Mum carried on, in her steely I-am-going-to-kill-you voice.

One look at her face (which matched the voice) and I knew she'd got me. Quick change of tactic needed here.

'It wasn't my fault, Mum. I had to take this video back to Sam's brother. I promised I would.'

'Pity you didn't ask.'

'You would have said I wasn't allowed.'

I noticed Peter was keeping his head really close to his food, probably so no one would see that he was grinning.

'That's not the point. Sneaking off like that is exactly the same as lying.'

'Sorry,' I mumbled. 'Anyway, what did Frankie want?'

It was a smart move asking that question because one: it would get us off the subject of me and the phantom bath, and two: it might give me a clue about Frankie. I needed all the clues I could get. I mean, I wasn't about to go round broadcasting it, but the thought of this holiday with two girls was scaring me to death. Charlie, the twelve-year-old, seemed all right – a bit bossy and far too chatty – but basically pretty normal. It was Frankie, the thirteener, I was worried about.

'She was actually phoning to speak to *me*. She wanted to find out whether she'd need to take any smart clothes on holiday,' said Mum.

Smart clothes? On a holiday? Do me a favour!

'What did you tell her?'

'I said it might be an idea to take one smartish pair of trousers or a skirt, just in case.'

'In case of what? You're not planning on taking us to any boring concerts, I hope!'

'We haven't planned anything, but if you play much more football in the next few days, you won't be taking any clothes at all because they'll all be in the wash.'

'That'd be good,' Rory giggled. 'Ollie in the nude. Bet Frankie'd love that.'

I rolled my eyes at the ceiling, pretending I thought Rory was stupid, but actually, he'd got me worried. I started imagining how awful it would be if Frankie suddenly came in to the bathroom and caught me starkers.

'Don't be silly,' said Mum.

And my stepdad Peter did the same look as I'd just done, to show that he agreed with me. He's great, Peter. He never really gets cross with me. When Mum tells me off he doesn't interfere. He just sits there quietly, and then finds a way to take her mind off the subject.

'So what did Frankie want to speak to *me* for?' I asked, looking out of the window as though I wasn't that interested really.

'She didn't say. She just asked if she could have a quick word with you.'

'Maybe she wanted to know if you were taking any make-up, Ollie,' giggled Rory.

'Excuse me while I die laughing,' I said, giving Rory my hardest look. But he'd got me imagining stuff again. I didn't like the thought of girly things like make-up all over the place.

'She'd better not be taking make-up,' I said, 'otherwise it'll take ten times longer to get ready to go out anywhere.'

'Don't exaggerate, Ollie,' said Mum. 'And stop complaining. It works both ways. Boys can be very irritating to girls too, you know.'

'What about clearing the table?' Peter suddenly changed the subject. 'It'll be good practice for when we're on holiday.'

And with that he leapt up and started rushing round, grabbing everyone's plates.

'Quite right. Up you get,' said Mum. 'When we're away, you boys must make sure you do at least as much helping as the girls.'

Mum's remark must have slipped into my subconscious because that night I dreamt that Frankie and Charlie were reclining on golden settees, wearing long flowing orange dresses and painting their toenails, while Peter, Rory and I waited on them hand and foot.

It was a nightmare, I can tell you.

3 GIRL POWER!
(THAT'S WHAT <u>THEY</u> THINK)

'Peter'll be back with Charlie and Frankie in about five minutes, you two,' Mum called up the stairs. 'Bring your bags down so we can load the car and set off straight away.'

'Can I have your mobile phone for the journey, Mum?' I called down to her.

'Whatever for?'

'I want to play that Snakes game on it.'

'Well, I don't mind you playing the odd game on it, but I don't want you ignoring Frankie, Ollie.'

'I'm not her personal entertainer, am I? I notice you don't tell Rory not to ignore Charlie.'

'Charlie's got a set of travel games for two people to play. She and Rory have been talking on the phone about it. I just don't want poor Frankie to be left out, that's all.'

Great! I thought. The holiday hasn't even started, and already Frankie's spoiling it.

As I was thinking that, I glanced through the hall window and saw the car backing into the drive. Frankie and Charlie were looking out of the rear window. I quickly ducked before they saw me.

It was a boiling hot day and it felt really stuffy in the car, but Peter had recently bought a People Carrier, so at least we weren't squashed. I'd wangled it so Charlie, Rory and Frankie sat together in the middle row and I sat behind them in the back. That meant I didn't have to talk to anyone, because it's really difficult to hear what people are saying when you're so far back.

I couldn't stop staring at Frankie and Charlie's long blonde hair. They looked pretty well identical from behind. Frankie was right in front of me. I'd never seen their hair at such close quarters before. It looked like dolls' hair, kind of shiny and wiry, and I kept getting this urge to touch Frankie's. At one point, when the others were deep into Travel Scrabble and Frankie was staring out of the window, I reached out to touch the ends, but at that very moment she suddenly swung round and asked me if I wanted to play twenty questions. I shook my head and pretended I was reading my comic, and luckily she turned round again pretty quickly, so I don't think she saw my red face.

We stopped in a lay-by at twelve o'clock. Everyone except Rory got out of the car to eat their sandwiches and crisps and stuff. Rory hardly ate a thing. He'd found my Game Boy and wanted as many goes on it as possible before we set off again.

'Come on, Rory,' said Peter after a while. 'Get out and stretch your legs.'

Rory took him literally and got Frankie to hold him under the arms while Charlie pulled his feet. He thought it was such a witty thing to do, poor, sad boy! It was the kind of thing Sam would have done. Which reminded me . . .

'Mum, did Mrs Cotteril phone you?'

'Yes,' said Mum, rolling her eyes. 'She wants us to meet up one day.'

'Who's Mrs Cotteril?' asked Charlie.

'She's Ollie's friend's mum.'

'Does that mean we're meeting your friend as well, Ollie?' asked Frankie.

'Dunno.'

'Yes, we are,' Mum told Frankie, giving me

a look that said, *Don't be so rude.*

'Oh great! What's his name?'

'Sam.'

'Has he got any brothers or sisters?' asked Charlie.

'One,' I told her.

'Sam's brother, Gareth, is twenty-one,' Mum explained, giving me another of her hard looks, 'so he's not going to North Devon. But apparently Sam and his mum are staying with Sam's auntie Letitia and her daughter, Daisy.'

'How old's Daisy?' asked Charlie.

'I think she's about your age.'

Oh, great!

When we got back in the car, Mum and Peter swapped places. Peter joked that Mum had to drive the last part because he didn't want her navigating when we got near to the place where we were staying.

'You know what your mum's like, boys. We

don't want to finish up in Wales, do we?'

'Peter, on the other hand, has got the most perfect map-reading skills,' Mum said. She was smiling. I *think* it was a joke.

The funny thing was that when we were within a few miles of the place, Peter's great skills went wrong and we got totally lost.

'You're hopeless, Dad,' said Frankie. 'Here, give me the map and the instructions.'

She read the instructions in about ten seconds and then studied the map for less than half a minute.

'Oh, I see where we've gone wrong. OK, Sue, take the next left and that should bring us out parallel with the road we took off the mini roundabout.'

I was gobsmacked by the way she'd sussed it so easily. She then proceeded to give Mum directions for the next five minutes. And what do you know, we were there!

'Brilliant, Frankie! Well done!' said Mum as she pulled up outside the house that was to be ours for the next fortnight. 'Girl power!'

I laughed. We all did because it sounded so weird hearing Mum use that expression.

'It's not very big,' said Rory, eyeing the house.

'I did warn you,' said Mum.

'It looks really sweet,' said Charlie. 'Lovely and cosy.'

And then a woman appeared from next door.

'Hello! You're early!' she said. 'You're lucky though. The last lot left at the crack of dawn, so it's all clean and ready for you.'

Mum thanked her and took the key.

'It's going to be great,' said Peter. 'The sun's shining, the birds are singing. We're twenty minutes from the beach. What more could we want?'

'Let's get going then,' I said.

'We've got to unpack first,' said Charlie.

'Yeah, let's do it as fast as we can and then go straight to the beach,' said Rory.

Huh! Fat chance of that happening with girls around.

'Peter and I have been driving for the last five and a half hours, you two. We don't really want to get in the car again straight away,' said Mum.

'I'll make you a nice cup of tea,' said Frankie, greasing up to Mum.

'What a lovely idea,' said Mum, giving Frankie her biggest smile.

I knew this would happen. The girls were taking Mum's side right from the word go. We three wouldn't stand a chance. The only good thing was that Charlie was very fast at taking her bags in. The moment she'd dumped them in the hall she went charging round the house calling out to the rest of us what every single room looked like before we got to it ourselves.

'The kitchen's lovely and big – microwave

and everything . . . the sitting-room's quite big too . . . telly's a bit small, but really comfy settees . . . Oh, can this be Frankie's and my bedroom? You can actually see the sea out of this window. Oh, double bed . . . right . . . Well, we'll have this room then. It's got pink in it, Rory. You'd hate it . . . The bathroom's nice . . . Oh no! The loo's in the bathroom! No, wait a minute, there's a separate loo here . . . And this bedroom'll be best for Ollie and Rory. The wardrobe's bigger than ours, but I don't like the carpet very much.'

'Got it sorted then?' Peter asked Charlie as he dumped his and Mum's suitcases on the double bed. 'How about seeing if the boys have got any views on the subject?'

'This bedroom will be OK for us two, won't it, Rory?' I said quickly.

I needn't have bothered to ask. Rory didn't care. He was already pulling clothes out of his bag and chucking them on the bed, in the room that Charlie wanted us to have.

'Hurry up, you two,' he called out to Mum and Peter. 'The sooner you sit down, the sooner the hour will be over.'

Mum laughed as she came upstairs. 'I didn't mean *exactly* an hour, Rory. I just don't want to hurry, that's all.' She poked her head round our door. 'And fold those clothes neatly and put them in the drawer.'

By the time Mum and Peter came downstairs, Frankie had unpacked everything that we'd brought for the kitchen and she'd even made tea and set it out properly on the table.

'How lovely! I can tell this is going to be a wonderful fortnight!' said Mum, smiling at Frankie and Charlie.

For *her* maybe. Not for me.

4 THE BIGGEST WAVE

At about three-thirty we packed all the beach things and set off. The roads were very narrow and winding so we had to go slowly. It seemed to take ages and I was boiling hot. I couldn't wait to go in the sea.

'It's busy, isn't it?' said Mum, looking at the crowded beach.

'Never mind, we'll find a little spot some-where, I'm sure,' said Peter.

Just then a whole family started to pack up their things about twenty metres away, so I ran on ahead and grabbed their place.

'This is perfect,' said Mum, smiling round happily as she slapped sun cream on to her legs a few minutes later. Charlie sat down next to her and did exactly the same thing. So far it was going just as I wanted. Mum and the girls would sunbathe while Rory, Peter and I would body-board and things.

I glanced over at Frankie. She had her back to the rest of us and was pulling the top half of her swimming costume up. I quickly pretended to be looking at something in the sand because I didn't want Rory piping up, *Ollie's staring at Frankie getting changed, Mum!* which was the kind of thing the little toerag would say just to wind me up. I did have another glance though.

'Come on, Peter, let's go and surf,' I said.

'Bit cold for me, Ollie,' said Peter, sitting down on the other side of Mum.

'Cold? It's boiling!'

'It might be boiling to you, Ollie, but we delicate grown-up people feel the cold more than you do,' joked Mum.

'Come on, Rory,' I said. But he was fishing around in one of the big plastic bags full of beach stuff.

'Where's the bucket and spade, Mum?' he asked, sounding frantic.

'Don't worry,' said Mum, 'it's in the other bag.'

'Aren't you coming into the sea?' I asked him.

'Nope. I'm going to build a castle with a moat round it. You can help if you want. Did you pack two spades, Mum?'

'I packed four actually,' said Mum.

I suddenly wished I was like Rory – a ten-year-old boy who didn't give a microchip about anything. And that's when the first shock of the day happened.

'I'll come in the sea with you, Ollie,' said

Frankie, fishing in one of the bags for something.

'Er . . . don't you want to sunbathe?' I asked her, praying that she'd say yes and stay with the others. I didn't want her coming into the sea with me. It wouldn't be the same. I mean, she was a girl! Well, more like a sister, I suppose. But then I didn't really know her properly. I wouldn't be able to muck about with her – not like I do with Rory or Sam.

'No, I want to go in the sea. Honestly,' she said, twisting her hair up on to the top of her head. This time it was impossible not to stare. I couldn't figure out how she was going to squash so much hair into one little hairband thing, but somehow it worked.

'Are you sure you're not just being kind to Ollie?' Mum asked her.

'No, I love the sea,' she answered.

Now what was I going to do? I looked at the

sea. The tide was pretty far out, which meant that it would take ages to get there. If it was Rory and me we'd run fast all the way, and splash each other in the rock pools. No way was I about to do that with Frankie! You never know with girls. She might go moaning back to Peter that I'd wet her hair or something.

'Come on. Race you!' Frankie grabbed one of the body boards and set off running. She left me standing there looking like a complete dork with my mouth hanging open.

Two boys who were probably a couple of years older than me walked past at that moment. They looked at Frankie then nudged each other and grinned. They must have thought she looked nice. I wondered if they reckoned she was my sister or my girlfriend or what. I suddenly realised I was still standing there, and Frankie was getting a bit too much of a start. Never mind, it wouldn't take long to catch her up.

Just as I was setting off with the other body board, she stopped.

'Keep going. I'll catch you up!' I called out.

But she just stood there waiting for me to work my way round all the people on the beach. When I drew level with her she broke into a run.

'I didn't want to have an unfair advantage,' she laughed.

Right, Frankie, if you want a race, you can have a race!

I put on a big spurt and overtook her almost immediately. Neither of us spoke for a while, but I knew she wasn't far behind because I could hear her pounding footsteps. After a minute the sweat was pouring down my back and my arm ached because the body board was so light that the wind kept forcing it sideways. I wished I could turn round to see how Frankie was coping with her board, but that would lose me time. I looked at the sea in the distance – there was still quite a way to go.

'Want to stop, Ollie?'

'What for?'

'I just wondered if you thought it was too hot for running.'

'No. You can, if you want.'

'No, I'm OK.'

Pity!

So on we ran, my legs feeling heavier and heavier with every footstep. I couldn't help slackening the pace a bit, and thank goodness, she did the same, so after another minute we were jogging along side by side. I hoped she'd forgotten it was a race. I hoped in vain, because as soon as we came to within a few metres of the sea, she suddenly put on a big spurt, kicking and splashing her way in, while I followed, trying to keep up. Then she chucked the body board to one side and dived under a wave.

'Think that makes me the winner,' she said a moment later, throwing her arms up to the sky and falling back into the sea, laughing. She was still laughing when she came up the second time. 'This is so brilliant, Ollie, isn't it?'

I didn't answer, just started looking for a really big wave. As she'd won the race, I wanted to make sure that at least I out-surfed her, otherwise she'd think I was a total nerd.

My luck was in. An enormous wave was gathering up right behind me. I'd body-surfed loads of times on holiday last year. You have to judge exactly the right moment to plunge forwards on to the board. I knew this was going to be a good one and I was right. It was spot on. The feeling you get when the wave scoops you up and sweeps you along is really great. It took me right to the shore.

'That was good, Ollie!' called Frankie. 'My go now.'

She didn't choose such a powerful wave as the one I'd chosen and she took off just a moment too soon, but still managed to come quite far.

'You're better at it than me. I plunged in too soon,' she said as she drew level with me. 'Let's have another go. It's great!'

But I was standing there with my mouth hanging open again, wasn't I? I just didn't get it. None of my friends would ever admit that I was better than them at anything – not even Sam. (And I suppose if I've got a best friend, it must be him, even though we don't have that much in common. He's pretty useless at sport but really good at everything else, and he's a great laugh.) So was it a girl thing, or was it just a Frankie thing?

We surfed for at least half an hour and it was the best fun I'd had in ages. Frankie got quite good at it and said we ought to try racing. I won nearly all the races but she didn't seem bothered.

On one race the wave shot my board right into her shoulder. She made a sort of gasping noise and I thought it must have really hurt her. She stood up and rubbed her arm, but I couldn't see her face because her hair had all fallen out of the thing on top of her head.

'Are you OK?'

'Yeah . . . thanks.'

I was amazed. I expected her to storm off in a big sweat but nothing else happened. Then Rory and Charlie appeared.

'Hi, you two. Can we have the boards for a while?' Charlie said.

It was only fair that we handed them over, but I felt a bit kind of lost with nothing to do except splash about. It would have been all right with Peter or Rory or one of my friends, but I wasn't sure what to do with Frankie. Last year on holiday Rory was always jumping on me, then he had to try and hang on while I used all my strength to try and chuck him off. It worked the other way round too, because of the water making you lighter. There was no way I could play that with Frankie because our bodies'd have to touch and that would have been far too embarrassing.

'I'll go back and get a ball and we can chuck it about in the sea,' Frankie suggested. 'Yeah?'

I couldn't believe my luck. She wanted to do all the things I thought she'd hate. It might be an idea if I got the ball myself though. If she told Mum or Peter about her shoulder, they'd try to get her to sit down for a while, and I'd have no one to muck about with. It was so odd that I was thinking like this. I never thought I'd find it a good laugh being with Frankie.

'I'll go,' I said.

But I was too late. She was already leaping through the waves, her knees and feet sticking out and kicking at odd angles. She really didn't care. I never knew girls acted like this.

Rory and Charlie were trying to stand on the body boards. They were laughing hysterically because they kept falling off. As Frankie passed them they called out to her, so she didn't notice those same two boys that I'd spotted looking at her earlier, running past. They both whistled loudly as she broke into a jog. She must have heard them, but she didn't turn round or anything. They stared at her for a while, then splashed their way into the sea. Something tightened inside me. I wasn't sure why, but I wished they hadn't whistled.

And that was when it hit me. Just like being knocked over by the biggest wave in the sea. I was jealous of those boys! I didn't want them looking at Frankie like that.

But then straight away afterwards there was this massive confusion inside my head because Frankie's my stepsister, and *step*sister is only a step away from *real* sister. Literally! And you don't get jealous because of your real sister, do you? So why was I jealous? I didn't get it. It was really doing my head in, all this step stuff.

5 RORY STARTS STIRRING

I sat bolt upright in bed. Something was wrong. What was Rory doing fast asleep in my room? Why were there two beds, anyway? I blinked about ten times to try and shake the sleep away, then I took a proper look round and realised where I was. Of course! We were on holiday. Great! No school, no work, just beach and . . .

That's when I remembered. Frankie.

I'd been thinking about the jealousy thing right up until bedtime the day before. And when I'd gone to bed, I couldn't get to sleep for ages because I was really worried. If I was jealous of those boys, I must fancy Frankie! It was totally gross. You can't fancy your own stepsister. She was practically my sister, for god's sake, so I had to get all those stupid thoughts out of my head once and for all. Trouble was, this was a brand new day and I didn't feel any different. How could I make the thoughts go away? They were stuck there.

I got out of bed and was about to get dressed when I found myself smelling my armpits.

Ollie, you nerd, what are you doing?

I'd only just told myself to get a grip when here I was sniffing my armpits. It was quite a good job I did though, because they were a bit pongy. I went into the bathroom to see if there was any deodorant. My luck was in. I sprayed it all over me for good measure, then went back to my room to get dressed.

I was just about to put yesterday's clothes on

when I stopped. I might look better in something different.

What! Are you out of your mind, Ollie? It was
happening again. Now I was even thinking what
Frankie might like me to be wearing. How
sad is that! I really had to put a stop to this
Frankiemania before it got out of control.

I grabbed yesterday's clothes and put them
on. Then I yanked back the curtains to check it
was going to be a good day for the beach.

The light streaming in made Rory grunt, but
he didn't wake up properly. I was just about to
whiz downstairs when I thought I saw some
Morse code flashes through the trees across the
road. I looked again and realised it was only the
sun glinting. Maybe I'd tell Frankie about it
though. In fact if she was awake I could even
show her. She'd appreciate that, I know, because
yesterday evening she'd made us all go to her
bedroom window and look at the sun setting.

'What are you smiling at?' Rory's squeaky morning voice interrupted my thoughts.

'I wasn't smiling.'

'Yes, you were. It looked really girly.'

I didn't bother to answer, just went downstairs. But I realised at that moment that I'd have to be very careful. My life wouldn't be worth living if Rory ever found out that I'd got a thing about Frankie. You see, Rory makes a point of noticing everything I say and do, then he jumps on the titchiest embarrassing thing and takes the mickey out of me to wind me up. (He's got this friend called Nick. Nick's got an older brother too, and I think Rory and Nick have got some kind of competition going to see who can get up their brother's nose the most.)

Right now, I need Rory around about as much as I need a broken leg. It feels like I'm under a magnifying glass. I'm going to have to make sure I don't even look at Frankie if Rory's anywhere within fifty metres. It's certainly not going to be a picnic, stuck in this little house.

'Mum, what day are we supposed to be meeting up with Sam and his parents?' I asked at breakfast time.

'I'd forgotten about that,' replied Mum, her voice going all flat. 'I said we'd meet them in Brinton on Thursday.'

'Who's Sam again?' asked Charlie.

'Ollie's weird friend,' Rory answered.

I didn't want Frankie to think I'd got any weird friends, but on the other hand, it was true. Sam *was* weird.

'There's nothing wrong with weird people,' said Frankie.

It sounded like she was sticking up for me, and before I realised it I found I was smiling at her. Big mistake that! Rory was wearing one of his lopsided grins so I knew he was about to do a bit of stirring. Pity I couldn't reach across the table and throttle the life out of him. Throttling was obviously out, but I had to do something quickly. Instead I stretched the smile into a sort of leer, went cross-eyed and waggled my head from side to side, so it looked as though I was taking the mickey out of Frankie for trying to be clever. Immediately her face fell and she went pink. I wanted to kick myself and then kick Rory for making me do that.

Frankie, still blushing, got up and took her plate and mug over to the sink.

'Come on, you two,' said Mum to Rory and me. 'Remember what we said about everyone helping.'

I leapt to my feet and made a lunge for the sink because there was a small shred of hope that I might be able to put things right with Frankie, out of earshot of everyone else.

'That's what he does – Sam,' I mumbled when I was right beside her, with our backs to the others.

'What?'

'That face and that waggling thing. He's always doing that. He's really weird!'

Frankie turned slowly to look at me. I think she was trying to search my expression to see whether or not I was joking. Her face was only about fifteen centimetres from mine and I could see the freckles on her nose and the way her eyelashes went straight down and didn't curl at all. Everything inside me knotted up and then came back to normal again. That had never happened before. It gave me a shock.

The first I knew that Rory had been creeping up on us was when his face suddenly popped up right between mine and Frankie's.

'Caught you!' he said in a sing-song voice.

'Don't be stupid,' I said, knowing that I was a bit pink. 'We were just –'

'What? Checking each other for zits?' said Rory, then he nearly fell over, laughing at his witty remark.

I expect the pink turned bright red, but with any luck I managed to hide it by making a dive for the pedal bin, whipping out the bin liner and going to the door.

'Well done, Ollie,' said Peter. 'The water down here must be doing you good. I've never known you empty a bin without being asked.'

'It's 'cos he's getting girly,' said Rory.

When I came back Rory decided to carry on with his stupid theme.

'This morning Ollie was smiling out of the window at the view. I mean, that's not normal, is it?'

'It was a really nice sunrise,' I mumbled, looking at my feet and feeling totally embarrassed, but desperately wanting Frankie to know that she wasn't the only one to appreciate that kind of thing.

When I looked up, I found that everyone was looking at me in a peculiar way, as though I'd started foaming at the mouth. I must have gone a bit too far with my sunrise remark. I'd have to tone it down a bit in future.

'Let's go the beach,' I changed the subject.

'Yes, we don't want to waste a single second of this glorious weather,' said Mum.

Phew! Close one!

6 SPIT!

We spent most of that day and the next two days on the beach. It was really weird because no matter what I was doing – surfing, swimming, playing Frisbee – my mind was on Frankie. I knew it was stupid but I kept imagining she was watching me. So say I was watching telly, I'd have to keep checking I hadn't got my mouth hanging open or anything, because if she happened to be looking at that moment, she'd think I was totally uncool. Things like picking your nose or even yawning were definitely out.

Sometimes I got mad at myself for having such pathetic thoughts, and then I'd start wondering what Frankie really thought about me. She probably didn't notice me – and even if she *did*, she probably couldn't care less what I looked like. But she did act as though she liked me a lot – I mean, much more than Rory. And it was true that she seemed to prefer being with me to being with Charlie. But that didn't mean anything, did it?

On Wednesday the weather broke. When I woke up and looked out of my window to find it all grey, I felt instantly depressed. It looked like the beach was out, which was gutting because that was one great place for getting away from Hawkeye Rory, and I'd got used to having Frankie all to myself in the sea.

'What shall we do today?' Frankie asked at breakfast time.

'What's wrong with the beach?' I asked as casually as I could, just in case by some miracle the others agreed.

'You're joking!' said Mum. 'We'd freeze on the beach.'

'Not if you do things,' I carried on desperately.

'Like what?' asked Peter.

'Play at Frisbee or ball or build sandcastles. It'd be a great day for building castles,' I told Rory, 'because there'd be hardly anyone about, so you could make the biggest sandcastle ever.'

And when we get there I'll soon convince Frankie that the sea feels warmer in the rain.

'Have you actually looked out of the window this morning, Ollie?' Peter asked me with a puzzled sort of grin.

I was just waiting for Rory to come out with some embarrassing comment, when Charlie suddenly said, 'I like it when it rains.'

'See!' I said, giving Peter a look. 'Not

everyone's as chicken as you and Mum.'

'I wasn't going to say that,' said Charlie. 'I was going to say, I like it when it rains because we can stay here and be all cosy together.'

Yuck! Not likely.

'You don't go on holiday to stay in all day,' I told her. 'What about Quasar Laser, Mum? Or an amusement arcade?'

'I think it would be a good chance to explore some of these pretty little coastal villages. Don't you, Peter?' said Mum.

'Maybe we should compromise – a bit of exploring and a bit of amusement arcade-type stuff.'

'Yeah, or a theme park,' I said, trying to get Mum away from her boring sightseeing idea.

'Yeah, a theme park!' said Frankie and Rory at exactly the same time.

And at that very moment there was a flash of lightning and a giant crack of thunder.

Frankie suddenly rushed over to Peter and he put his arm round her. 'Frankie's never liked storms,' he explained to the rest of us, while she kept her face hidden.

'*I* love them!' said Charlie, rushing to the front door to look at the sky.

I was thinking what a shame the others were all there. If it had just been Frankie and me, *I* would have had to put my arm round her. Not Peter. My stomach did that tightening thing again at the thought of her being that close to me.

'Let's get into teams and have a games tournament while it's raining,' said Charlie, 'then go out later. We brought quite a few games, didn't we, Sue?'

'Well, we've got two packs of cards and a ludo board,' said Mum.

All our names were put in a tin, then Rory read out the pairs for the teams. It came out that he and I were together, Frankie and Mum were together, and Charlie and Peter.

Just my luck! Let's hope we can get the whole thing over and done with pretty fast, then go out somewhere.

I watched Charlie and Frankie marking out the big score sheet, their heads together as they leaned over the table. I'd seen Rory and Charlie with their heads like that when they'd been digging in the sand, so nobody would think it weird if Frankie and I got that close. If Rory dared to say anything I'd turn to Frankie and say, *Sorry about my little brother. He's going for the Idiot of the Year award.* Yeah, that would be good. She'd find that really witty.

Rory taught us all how to play this mega-fast card game called Spit. Only two people can play at once so whoever wasn't playing, played a quick version of ludo. I didn't get to play Frankie at Spit until the very end of the whole tournament.

'If Frankie wins this, her team has won the whole thing, but if Ollie wins, that makes *us* two the winners,' Rory said, practically jumping up and down with excitement. 'So come on, Ollie!' he added, slapping me on the back.

'Come on, Frankie!' said Mum, getting pretty excited (for her) too.

'Right,' said Peter, 'this is serious stuff. You'd better shake hands, you two, before you start.'

My eyes met Frankie's as our hands touched and I went all kind of dizzy. Something must have shown in my face because Rory suddenly cupped his hand round his mouth and whispered in my ear, 'You fancy Frankie, don't you?'

I felt like whacking him one, but I knew I had to stay cool otherwise he'd know he'd hit the nail on the head, and that would be the pits. So I gave him a *stop being so pathetic* look and started laying out the cards.

'One, two, three, go!' said Mum when we were both ready.

'Come on, Ollie!' Rory screeched in my ear.

I was going much faster than Frankie and I reckoned I could easily beat her, but I'd feel really sorry for her if she didn't win, because she'd think she was letting Mum down.

'Come on, Frankie!' said Mum.

I glanced at the cards on Frankie's side of the table. She still had loads left to turn over and I'd only got a few. I had to do something drastic or I'd win at any moment. Then poor Frankie would have to suffer Rory crowing about us two being the winners. And then Mum would make it worse by coming out with something diplomatic about how it was only luck anyway, when it was perfectly obvious it was a game of skill.

I couldn't bear it any longer. I deliberately dropped one of my cards on the floor and then spent ages pretending to try and pick it up off the carpet.

'I'll get it, Ollie, you wally,' said Rory diving under the table. 'You get on with the game. You dropped that card on purpose.'

'No, I didn't,' I snapped back at him, but my cheeks felt hot.

'Yes, you did,' said Rory. 'You've gone all red again. That proves it.'

Frankie was piling on the cards quite quickly now. Good. I only needed to hang on playing dumb for another few seconds and she'd win.

'It's not fair!' screeched Rory. 'He's going slow on purpose.' Then he turned to Peter. 'This game doesn't count, does it?'

'Out!' cried Frankie, clapping her hands together.

She jumped up and gave Mum a big hug, then they started dancing round together like a pair of schoolgirls. 'We won! We won!'

'It wasn't fair,' repeated Rory through his black scowl. 'Ollie deliberately let her win.'

'Don't be silly,' said Mum. 'It's only a game.'

'He's in love with her,' Rory went on in his big mocking voice. 'Anyone can see that.'

I went even brighter red.

'Course I'm not. I just felt sorry for her, because she's no good at Spit,' I said.

The moment the words were out of my mouth, I could have kicked myself. Frankie turned on me. I could see tears in her eyes.

'I don't need your sympathy, Ollie,' she said very quietly.

I got up and went out of the room, because it felt like my face had won the reddest tomato of the year competition. Rory, the toerag, followed me all the way upstairs.

'I'm going to the toilet, Rory. Do you want to come too?' I asked sarcastically.

'I just came to tell you that whatever you say,

I *know* you're in love with her, because I've heard you saying her name in your sleep. It's so embarrassing.'

'Well, it must have been a nightmare if I did,' I snapped back at Rory.

Then just when I was on the point of going into the toilet, I saw that Frankie had appeared at the top of the stairs. She must have heard every word.

7 PIGGY IN THE MIDDLE

It didn't take Einstein to work out that Mum had told Rory to get off my case. Ever since the red tomato competition, whenever Mum was around, he acted like he was going for best behaved boy of the year. But the moment we were on our own, he pretended to be playing romantic violin music, giving it the full smoochy sound effects, or otherwise he made some clever little remark like, 'Oh, where's your girlfriend, Ollie? Better find her quick in case she's missing you.'

'Don't be stupid, Rory. She's practically my sister,' I'd snap back at him.

Because of my pathetic little brother, everything had gone wrong. Before he'd started interfering, Frankie and I had been getting on really well together. Now she was all distant and unfriendly. It was unbearable.

On the afternoon of the tragic tournament, we went for miles in the car. Twice we stopped to explore little coastal villages. The pavements were always too narrow for more than two people to walk side by side. I happened to be next to Charlie for quite a while. She did that thing of not stepping on the cracks between the paving stones, but they were a bit too close together, so she had to take stupid little mincing steps. She pretended to be a posh girl wiggling her hips and I couldn't help laughing. But then I felt suddenly sad. I wished it was Frankie and me laughing.

The following day I woke up and remembered this was the day we were going to meet Sam. It was going to be so weird having Sam around at the same time as Frankie. I wasn't sure that I was looking forward to it. Normally I'd be really pleased about the thought of having a laugh with my best mate, but everything was different now. I just wanted to be with Frankie and no one else.

We were due to meet Sam and his mum outside Marks and Spencer's in Brinton at 12.30 and then eat dinner with them, somewhere like McDonald's hopefully. We were a bit late so I guessed they'd get there first. I guessed right.

We all spotted Mrs Cotteril from miles away. She was wearing a bright pink jacket on top of a pair of black shiny trousers with enormous flares. On her head was a whopping great floppy straw hat, and perched on her nose a pair of very little round sunglasses. When you got nearer you could see that her shirt was white with pink spots on it, and the top bit turned into a sort of floaty scarf. Then when you got even nearer you could see little stiletto heels poking out from the bottom of the trousers. What did she think she looked like! I didn't know how Sam could bear to be seen with her. I'd have to stand a few metres away from Mum if she ever dressed like that.

'Coo-eee!' she called, waving both arms in the air as though she was flagging in a Boeing 747.

I noticed poor old Sam trying to grab one of her arms to stop her, but she just shook him off and kept waving.

'Good old Pammy!' said Mum.

'What *have* I let myself in for?' muttered Peter.

Rory giggled and turned to Charlie and Frankie. 'Told you Sam was weird, didn't I?

Well, now you know where he gets it from.'

Frankie laughed loudly. She wasn't so quick to defend weird people this time, I noticed.

'Hi, Sam. Hello, Mrs Cotteril,' I said.

'Ollie, you must call me Pammy. Are you having a lovely holiday? *We* are, although we've left my sister Letitia and my niece at home. Poor Daisy isn't feeling a hundred per cent today. Still, never mind. I expect you'll meet her another day.'

Sam rolled his eyes at me, as Mum and the others arrived. Sam's mum was staring at Frankie and Charlie with this really silly smile on her face, even though she was talking to Mum.

'Hello, Sue. You're looking tanned. Not good for you, you know. It'll ruin your skin, not to mention the health hazard. But it *does* suit you, my dear, I must confess. And who are these two lovely young ladies?'

'This is Frankie and this is Charlie,' said

Mum. But Mrs Cotteril was nodding and waiting for more.

'Peter's daughters,' Mum explained.

Frankie and Charlie smiled dutifully.

'Hello, my dears.'

'You've met Peter before, haven't you, Pammy?' said Mum.

'Oh yes, yes yes,' said Mrs C, wafting her hand about as though she was trying to get rid of Mum's silly remark. 'We met at the school fête, didn't we, Peter? I was the one serving the squash, remember?'

Peter smiled and mumbled something.

'Come on, then,' she said, as she swung round, narrowly missing Rory's head with her handbag. (Pity.) Then she went striding through the crowded street, like a big pink plough, while we all followed meekly. 'I've found us the most super little restaurant within walking distance, and booked a table . . .' She stopped without warning to look at her watch, and Muggins went into the back of her. I could hear Sam sniggering and the others trying to hide their giggles. Great start! Mrs Cotteril didn't appear to notice, and I must admit her back felt very spongy. Perhaps she wore body protection. 'Twelve thirty-five. Perfect timing.' Then off she went again, left right, left right.

The restaurant was really posh.

'Mum always chooses places like this,' said Sam in a whisper to me. It was amazing that he didn't care. If it had been my mum I would have been dead embarrassed if we went anywhere that looked much different from McDonald's.

I saw Mum give Peter a worried look. I knew why. She was feeling anxious that it might be too expensive. She opened her mouth to say something, then shut it again and shrugged as Mrs Cotteril marched up to a waiter and told him she'd booked a table for twelve forty-five.

Our table was right in the middle of the whole restaurant. We were on the point of sitting down, when the foghorn started laying down the law.

'Come on, you two. You're not going to leave these beautiful young ladies with no young men to sit next to, are you? Let Frankie pop in next to you, Sam . . .'

Sam looked as though the thought of sitting next to Frankie was the scariest thing ever. He wasn't used to girls any more than I was, and I knew he'd hate having to sit next to her. I was praying that Mrs C would suggest that *I* should sit next to her instead, but I was out of luck.

'I'm fine, honestly,' said Frankie.

'Nonsense. Move up one, Sam.'

Sam stayed glued to me but shoved me along one, so Frankie could sit in the seat between him and Peter.

Mrs Cotteril was smiling and patting the chair next to her. 'You come and sit next to me, Sue. I want to hear what you've been getting up to.'

Mum was staring at the pepper like she was willing it to give her a bit of help. She needn't have bothered. Sam's mum was beaming round at us all.

'Lovely!' she said, taking her jacket off. 'Just how it should be – boy, girl, boy, girl . . . apart from those two naughty boys sitting together over there.'

'That's because of those two naughty girls sitting together over there,' said Charlie, pointing to Mrs Cotteril and Mum.

Peter closed his eyes as though he couldn't bear to see what was going to happen after his daughter's cheeky remark. Mrs Cotteril's eyes bulged. I don't suppose anyone had ever dared to speak to her like that before. We all held our breath and after a couple of seconds she suddenly let out a great guffaw of laughter and wagged her finger at Charlie.

'I can see you're going to be a terror!' she exclaimed, which made Rory break into uncontrollable giggles.

But the moment passed quickly. Mrs C held her pink jacket aloft.

'Waiter!' In about two seconds a waiter appeared and took the jacket. 'You can always tell how good a restaurant is by the attitude of the waiters, you know,' she whispered to Peter. She'd swapped her sunglasses for a pair of half glasses hanging on a sparkling string. She looked over the top of them at Mum.

'This meal is on me, my dear.' Mum started to protest, but Mrs Cotteril flapped Mum's words away again. 'No, no, no. I'm having none of it. I want to treat you all because I have a favour to ask you.' I saw Mum gulp. 'There's an absolutely super concert on tomorrow afternoon at the Dominion, and my sister's next-door neighbour's brother-in-law is the conductor, which is so exciting. Of course the youngsters would frankly be bored to tears. So . . . we were wondering whether you and Peter might be so kind as to have Sam and Daisy for us.'

'Yes, of course we will,' Mum said immediately. She looked quite relieved. She must have been imagining a much bigger favour.

'Jolly good. That's settled, then. Daisy will be fine tomorrow. She's had a touch of sickness and diarrhoea but nothing to worry about.'

'What's Daisy like?' Frankie asked Sam.

'She's all right,' Sam muttered, then he buried his head in the menu.

'Yes, but what's she *like*?' Frankie persisted.

'She's got short hair,' said Sam. This time he practically turned his back on Frankie, he was so embarrassed about talking to a girl. It was quite funny really.

'How old is she and what kind of things does she like doing?' Frankie leaned forwards and a big strand of her hair fell over Sam's shoulder. I saw him look at it out of the corner of his eye, and then try to pull his shoulder away subtly.

'Thirteen. Hockey,' was all he managed.

On the other side of me Charlie and Rory were giggling together about something – probably Sam.

'And what about you?' Frankie said to Sam, touching his arm for a second, to try and get him to face her a bit more, but it just made him jump.

Just then Peter chipped in.

'What shall we do tomorrow then, you lot? Got any ideas, Sam?'

Sam looked at Peter as though he'd just saved him from a man-eating alligator. 'Ten-pin bowling?' he piped up.

Yeah! That would be great.

'Ten-pin bowling?' said Peter. 'You any good at it, Sam?'

'He's a super little bowler!' said Mrs Cotteril, which made Charlie's menu shake up and down in front of her face, but Mrs C didn't even notice.

'Right, bowling it is,' said Peter. 'We'll have boys against girls.'

'And we'll slaughter them, won't we, girls?' said Mum.

'Yeah!' said Charlie, showing a pink face and watering eyes. I was right. She'd been having hysterics behind her menu.

'Whereabouts in Brinton are you staying, Sam?' Frankie went on, tossing her head so her hair went back over her shoulder.

And I suddenly got that same feeling that I'd had when those two boys had looked at her on the beach. I knew it was stupid, because it was only Sam, but I couldn't help feeling jealous.

Frankie was being so friendly with him, and I knew he'd start to get used to it after a bit. Then it was anyone's guess what might happen. If Frankie carried on draping her hair all over him, he might get the idea she fancied him. The very thought of that made my blood boil.

I wished we could get this stupid meal over with, and go home. Then I remembered about having to see him the next day. The whole thing was turning into a nightmare. If only Frankie would stop giving Sam so much attention! It was like she was doing it on purpose.

'That's a very fierce scowl, Oliver,' Mrs Cotteril suddenly broke off what she was saying to Mum to tell me.

I was already pretty mad, but that did it. It was bad enough having all these mixed-up feelings about Frankie, but I didn't want the whole world clocking every single expression I ever wore.

Good old Peter said something about Rory

and Charlie's sandcastles then, and it got Mrs Cotteril off my case.

But I could see Sam getting more and more mesmerised by Frankie's hair. Pity she hadn't got it up in one of those big scrunchie things. He finally stopped gawping and answered her question.

'At my Aunt Letitia's. She's divorced, you see.' He made it sound a really terrible thing to be. Frankie was nodding sympathetically, as though he'd just said she was terminally ill or something. Sam *did* have a dad, but he wasn't around much because he worked abroad.

'Loads of people are divorced these days,' I informed Sam.

'So whereabouts does Aunt Letitia live?' Frankie carried on, ignoring me.

She and Sam were acting like I wasn't there. Maybe I'd died without realising it, and turned into a ghost.

'She's got a flat in Duke Street. Number 4. She lives on the second floor. You have to take the lift.'

He'd be giving her his phone number next, the plonker!

After that, things went downhill all the way. All that I'd imagined, started coming true. Frankie talked more and more to Sam until he wasn't nervous of her at all. He was looking right into her eyes and cracking all sorts of clever jokes, while she giggled and looked at him from under her straight eyelashes. I nearly threw up.

To make matters worse, while those two were talking like mad on one side of me, Charlie and Rory were giggling like mad on the other side. I felt like poor sad piggy in the middle. Mrs Cotteril kept on trying to draw me into the adults' conversation, which stopped me from being able to hear what Frankie and Sam were saying to each other, and that made me more jealous than ever. I don't know why I ever thought Sam was my best mate. He certainly wasn't any more.

8 SCHEMING

It came as a big relief when Mrs Cotteril looked at her watch and said, 'Oh my goodness, three-thirty! How time flies when you're enjoying yourself.'

She paid the bill and we all thanked her very much.

'Oh no, no, no! It's *I* who must thank *you* for looking after the young folk tomorrow. Waiter?'

We followed her out of the restaurant and stood in a queue waiting to be kissed on both cheeks. There was no way out of it. She'd done it to Mum, Peter and Frankie so far. Talk about embarrassing! When it got to my turn I braced myself and turned my head really far to the side so her lips wouldn't reach properly. My technique worked: I was the only one who didn't have to rub the greasy pink mark off my face when she'd gone.

''Bye, Frankie,' said Sam in a gooey voice.

'See you tomorrow, Sam,' Frankie replied, tipping her head on one side and flashing him one of her really nice smiles.

Sam looked as though the Angel Gabriel had appeared and pronounced him the chosen one. It was amazing that one girl could have this effect. Not only had she got Sam *and* me thinking she was the greatest thing on God's earth, she'd got me hating my friend's guts too. Maybe that's what girl power means.

'Bye Sam,' I said loudly to bring him back to earth, but his eyes were still glued to Frankie.

'Yeah, seeya, Ollie.'

Not if I can help it!

From that moment on I was determined that somehow or other I was going to make sure that tomorrow afternoon never happened. I just couldn't stomach spending another second with Sam and Frankie hitting it off so brilliantly while I felt like a spare part. I spent the rest of the afternoon scheming. By the time we got back home I reckoned I'd come up with something that, with a bit of luck, would work a treat. I was going to pretend to be ill.

Next I had to decide on the illness. I didn't want to get everyone so worried that they started calling doctors or ambulances or anything like that, because I reckoned medical people would click there was nothing wrong with me pretty quickly. On the other hand I needed to be ill enough for Mum and Peter to be pretty anxious and feel very sorry for me. The good thing about this idea was that Frankie would be sorry for me too – so sorry that she'd forget all about my ex-friend Sam Cotteril.

Right, what was the illness to be? Food poisoning was probably the best idea because I could blame it on the meal we'd had in that posh restaurant. Except I wasn't sure when the poisoning would have started. Maybe I should wait till just after the pizza and chips that Mum was about to pull out of the freezer. No, that wouldn't work. With two large pizzas between six of us, the others would be poisoned as well.

I racked my brains to think of a solution, and it was Charlie who gave me my next bit of inspiration.

'I'm really full, Sue. I don't think I can manage pizza and chips after that big lunch and the ice cream in the park.'

'Yeah, I'm full too, Mum,' I said. 'Why don't

we just have sandwiches in front of the telly? I don't mind making them.'

Mum beamed at me. *Ten out of ten, Ollie.*

'Good idea, Ollie. Go for it!' She frowned. 'Wait a minute, what have we got to put in sandwiches?'

'We've got eggs and cheese and jam, haven't we?' I pointed out helpfully. 'I'll just make a selection,' I offered. 'How long are you supposed to boil the eggs for?'

'Turn the heat down when the water's boiled and leave them in for about ten minutes to be sure. Then put them in cold water to cool down before you shell them.'

As I went through to the kitchen I felt like singing because Frankie had almost smiled at me. At this rate I wouldn't need to be ill. I'd just keep impressing her with my helpful-boy-of-the-century act. My plan was to hardboil two eggs so there wouldn't be many egg sandwiches.

I'd do a lot more cheese and jam ones, but only eat the egg ones myself. That way, it would be perfectly possible that one of the eggs was rotten and that by coincidence I'd just happened to be the only one to eat sandwiches made from that egg. Brilliant! And utterly foolproof. I *did* start singing then, I felt so good.

'There you go,' I said a bit later, as I put the big silver platter down on the coffee table.

They were all engrossed in the television, but Mum gave me a nice smile and mouthed *Well done.*

I was hoping that Frankie might give me a nice smile too, but she just looked irritated because I was blocking the screen from her view. Talk about gratitude. Huh!

I quickly took three egg sandwiches and put them on my plate, then I thought I ought to draw attention to what I was eating, so that when I started writhing round with stomach cramps in about twenty minutes, everyone would instantly make the connection.

'Don't nick all the egg ones,' said Rory, who'd been the only one paying more attention to the sandwiches than to the telly.

The perfect opening. Cheers, Rory.

'Anyone want some tea?' I asked when all the sandwiches had gone.

'Yes please,' said Mum, with another big beam.

Peter winked at me and Charlie pretended to faint.

'No thanks,' said Frankie. 'But I'll help you make it if you want.'

It was like a nature reserve inside my stomach, there were so many butterflies belting about.

'Thanks.'

She followed me into the kitchen and we started getting all the tea things out, neither of us speaking. I wished I could get inside her head and find out whether she was thinking about Sam or me or what. This was the perfect situation to start acting ill, but I felt nervous all of a sudden. I didn't like the idea of deceiving Frankie. Still, it was all in a good cause.

'Aargh!'

'What . . .?'

I gripped the sink with both hands and lowered my head.

'Are you all right?'

'Yeah . . . yeah . . . I'll be OK. It felt like stomach cramp . . . Aargh!'

I made that second cry a bit more dramatic, but I didn't clutch my stomach or anything. I wanted to bring it on gradually.

'Are you all right in there?' called Mum from the other room.

'Ollie's got stomach cramp,' Frankie called back.

No one came rushing to my aid, I noticed.

It's great having such a loyal fan club!

I poured the boiling water on to the tea and deliberately made my hand shake as I was doing it. Out of the corner of my eye I could see the worried look on Frankie's face.

'You'd better sit down, Ollie. I'll finish off the tea.'

I went through to the other room then staggered past Mum, murmuring that I was going to the toilet.

She didn't say anything, but looked pretty concerned. So far, so good.

While I was in the bathroom I ran the hot water and hung my face over the rising steam with a towel over my head, for ages. When I looked in the mirror it looked just right. I'd got a sort of sweaty red glow. I belted downstairs really quickly before it went, then slowed right down for my entrance into the living-room. It still wasn't quite time to clutch my stomach, but I thought a bit of reeling around on my way to the settee would be good.

'I was nearly sick,' I told Mum weakly as I flopped back on to the settee.

That got her attention. She sat up quickly and examined my face carefully.

'My God, you're sweating, Ollie!'

'You look terrible!' Charlie added, screwing up her face into a disgusted expression.

'Have you still got stomach cramps?' asked Frankie.

I nodded and closed my eyes as though the pain was too much to bear.

Rory wasn't saying anything, I noticed, which either meant that he was so worried about his dearly beloved brother that he'd been rendered speechless, *or* he wasn't convinced by my act and he was watching me like a hawk, ready to bust my cover at the first opportunity.

Still, so far so good.

9 SICK!

I hadn't felt such power since I'd broken my arm in the school playground and all the teachers had gathered round me and spoken in gentle, caring tones. I had to be careful though. If I got sussed, I'd have to suffer watching Sam and Frankie hitting it off like Prince Charming and Cinderella, *and* get a load of grief from Mum.

Mum kept on reaching out to feel how hot I was.

'That's better,' she said after a while. 'You

don't seem to have such a temperature now. I was quite worried there for a while.'

And that got *me* worried. I didn't want to overdo it and pretend to be sick too often, or I'd get sussed, but on the other hand, I had to appear to be ill enough to cock up the arrangements for the next day, I reckoned another trip to the bathroom was about due.

'I feel sick again!' I said, making a dive for the door and rushing upstairs.

I ran another basin full of really hot water and went through the towel routine again to get that sweaty look back, then I was ready.

'Have you been sick?' asked Mum sympathetically when I reappeared.

I wasn't sure if Mum would take one sniff and know straight away that I was lying, so I knew I had to be careful.

'A bit,' I answered in a whisper as I sunk dramatically into the settee.

'You'd better try and drink a bit of water,' said Mum. 'You must be quite dehydrated.'

I sipped at the water but kept my eyes shut as though I was exhausted. Actually, I *was* exhausted. It wasn't easy keeping the act up with so many people watching me. Rory looked as though he wasn't quite convinced, for a start. But I knew how my little brother's mind worked. He'd be thinking that he'd better not accuse me of faking it, just in case he was wrong, because then everyone would hate him for being so hard on me.

I was also knackered because of trying to keep an eye on Frankie without anyone noticing. The last thing I wanted was to make her go off me even more, but it's not easy to look burning hot *and* super-cool at the same time. I kept my eyes closed because I had the horrible feeling Rory was trying to catch me out. I wished he'd just go to bed or something.

'What are we going to do if Ollie's still not well tomorrow?' Charlie asked the six million dollar question.

'We'll cross that bridge when we come to it,' Mum replied. 'I think you should go to bed now, love,' she said to me, stroking my hair off my face.

I felt pretty smug as I lay in bed, staring into the darkness. I just had to show no signs of improvement in the morning, and hopefully the whole trip would be called off. I could hear them all killing themselves laughing at something on the telly, and I wished I was down there too, but I reckoned it was worth giving up one evening to make sure I didn't have to suffer the company of Romeo and Juliet the next day.

I was suddenly aware of whispering and tiptoeing around me. I listened for a while with my eyes closed, while the memory of the previous evening slowly came back to me. We'd finally arrived at that awful day. I gave a little moan and turned over.

'How do you feel?' asked Mum, sitting on my bed and stroking my forehead. 'I don't think you've got a temperature, so that's a good start.'

'My head aches,' I whispered, 'and so does my stomach.'

I half opened my eyes and saw that Rory and Charlie were hovering in the doorway, waiting for the verdict.

'Do you want to get up and see how you feel, love?'

'I'll try,' I said, wishing that Rory and Charlie would go away. It was so much easier fooling Mum on her own.

'I'll be downstairs. Just call out if you want me.'

She shooed Rory and Charlie away as she went out, but I made sure I got out of bed very slowly and with a pained expression on my face just in case Antennae Features was peeping through the crack in the door. When I went to the bathroom I could hear that they were all talking in hushed voices downstairs but I couldn't make out what they were saying. I looked in the mirror and thought I looked far too healthy and normal. I went back to bed and got down under the covers so that only the top half of my face was showing, then I called out to Mum in a really pathetic voice.

She came running up straight away and sat down on the bed.

'I tried getting up, Mum, but I haven't got any energy. I think it's because I was sick once more in the night. I'll be OK by tomorrow, but I'd better stay in bed today.'

'OK, love. You know how you feel. I'll stay with you.'

'What do you mean?'

'Don't worry about me, Ollie. I wasn't all that bothered about going bowling anyway. The others can go on their own and I'll have some time to myself for quiet reading. I'm looking forward to it. Honestly.'

She was nodding and smiling brightly to reassure me that she really didn't mind having to drop out of the great outing to the Brinton Bowlplex. And I was lying there, my brain in overdrive trying to think how I could rewind the morning and wake up again, miraculously cured. I wanted to kick myself for being such a dur. I should have realised they'd all just go bowling anyway, shouldn't I?

I couldn't bear the thought of Sam and Frankie there without me. Her eyelashes'd be batting so much, she'd probably get eye ache – and as for Sam, well, he'd just act like a complete idiot. I had to do something. And quick.

'Well, I might feel better by this afternoon.

We're not meeting them till then, are we?'

'No, but Peter thought it would be nice to have a look round the town beforehand and maybe get a McDonald's at lunchtime.'

What was she trying to do, torture me?

'I'm just going to the loo, Mum.'

I got out of bed slowly and went off to the bathroom. Then I cleaned my teeth and washed my face. By the time I got back to my room Mum was downstairs. I got dressed and went down too.

'I feel miles better now I've had a wash,' I said, smiling round at everyone.

'That's good,' said Peter. 'By tomorrow you'll be completely cured I should think. Just take it easy today. Your body must be quite weakened with all that vomiting.'

'Well, it was only twice and the second time there was hardly anything.'

'Lovely, Ollie!' said Rory, who was in the

sitting-room eating a piece of toast and kicking a ball of screwed-up newspaper round the room. 'Why don't you give me all the gory details, so I can *really* enjoy this toast.'

I ignored him.

'It's amazing. The weakness seems to have gone now,' I said, as I went through to the kitchen. 'Is there any toast left, Mum?'

'Are you sure you feel like eating, Ollie?'

'Yeah! I'm starving,' I grinned.

'You *are* feeling better!' She turned to Peter. 'I think as long as he takes it easy, he'll be all right to come along, don't you?'

'If Ollie thinks he can cope, I'm sure he can.'

Phew!

10 BOWLED OVER!

We weren't due to meet Sam and Daisy until two-thirty so we went out for the morning to a town about five miles away, where they had crazy golf, pedalos and various rides. We had a brilliant time – correction, everyone else had a brilliant time. I'd only been allowed to come on condition that I didn't do any of the white-knuckle rides. I begged and begged to be allowed to go in a bumper car and said I was feeling loads better, but Mum still wouldn't let me. The biggest torture was watching Frankie and Charlie going down this massive slide together in a sack, laughing their heads off. A few days ago that would have been Frankie and me.

Someone next to me said, 'Look at those pretty blonde girls. Do you think they're twins?' I felt proud for a moment that they were my stepsisters, and then I felt all confused again because I wished that Frankie could be my girlfriend.

The miracle happened when she said she'd ride in the ghost train with me. It was wicked because twice she grabbed hold of me when something scary suddenly jumped out at us. I nearly put my arm round her but I thought that might be overdoing it a bit. I wasn't sure if it was OK for a stepbrother to do things like that. I wanted to suggest that we had another go in the ghost train, but I could just hear Rory's scornful voice . . . *Ollie got better quickly, didn't he?*

When we got to the Bowlplex there was no sign of Sam and Daisy. Maybe they wouldn't show up at all. (Yeah, right. And maybe Brinton Bowlplex would freeze over.) Peter bought the tickets and we changed into bowling shoes and went to our lane. The man at the desk had asked us if we wanted bumpers up the sides of the lane. Mum said she thought it might be an idea as Charlie, Frankie and Rory had never played before, and I'd only played once, but we'd all insisted that we weren't babies and that we *did* know how to roll the balls accurately down the middle.

Frankie and Charlie were engrossed in setting up all the names on the computer screen that kept the score.

'How shall we organise the teams, Sue?' asked Frankie.

And that was when we heard, 'Cooo-eeeee!'

We turned to see Mrs Cotteril in a bright

green trouser suit that was even bigger and floatier than yesterday's clothes. Standing next to her was a lady with white-blonde hair that looked as though it had been pasted on to the top of her head in thick chunks. She was just as huge as Sam's mum and was wearing a big gold jacket and loads of gold jewellery.

She must be Mrs Cotteril's sister, I thought. *Poor old Sam, having to walk round with two of them like that!*

'They look like a pair of Spanish galleons in full sail,' Peter whispered in a voice just loud enough for all of us to hear.

Mum cracked up and then had to make out that it was a fit of coughing. The rest of us sniggered and pretended to be concentrating on the score screen. When we turned back round Sam and this gorky looking girl were approaching us, while Sam's mum jabbed her watch then held up five fingers and a thumb.

She was obviously coming back at six o'clock.

Mum gave her the thumbs-up sign, then the Spanish galleons waved and departed.

'Hello, you must be Daisy,' said Mum, because Sam wasn't bothering to introduce her. He was asking about the teams, like it was the draw for a cup final.

'You need to change your shoes, Sam,' Frankie told him. 'I'll take you.'

'I – oh, thanks!'

He was about to say *I know* but he changed his mind so that he could go with Frankie.

Here we go!

I watched them walk over to the desk. Frankie's hair was half up and half down, the way I liked it best. There was something different about Sam and I wasn't sure what it was at first.

'This is Daisy,' Mum said, smiling at Charlie and me.

'Hello,' we all said.

I couldn't believe that Daisy was thirteen. She looked like an oversized nine-year-old. She kind of bunched up her shoulders and tucked her head in, like a tortoise. She'd got very pink shiny cheeks and short hair.

'I'll take you to change your shoes,' said Charlie.

What a relief. I wouldn't have had a clue what to say to Daisy if it had been me. We'd have walked in silence all the way to the desk and all the way back. I noticed that she'd put lipstick on and she'd got glitter all round her eyes. I suppose I could have said something like, 'Oh, I see you've got glitter on,' but then she'd have said, 'Yes', and that would have been the end of that.

The sight of Sam and Frankie coming back really *did* make me feel like throwing up. Sam was kind of bobbing up and down in his brand new jeans, and both of them were chatting like they had to say as much as possible in sixty seconds. Maybe they'd sussed me and were laughing together about what a dweeb I was, fancying my own stepsister.

'How yer doing, Ollie?'

I didn't bother to reply because it was obvious he wasn't interested in how I was doing. It didn't even sound like Sam talking. He was trying to be so cool.

'Right, let's get these teams organised,' said Peter, as Daisy and Charlie came back. 'Shall we toss a coin?'

I held my breath and prayed. And that was a waste of time because it came out that I was with Charlie, Mum and Daisy. Great! So the other team was Peter, Rory, Frankie and Sam. I was definitely going to suggest swapping the teams round for the next game.

Rory went first and his ball missed the skittles

altogether and rolled down the dip at the side of the lane.

'I knew we should have had bumpers,' said Mum.

'That was only my first go. I'll be fine,' said Rory.

Everyone had two goes. Rory's second one wasn't much better – three skittles.

Next it was Charlie because we were going from youngest to oldest. Like Rory, she missed all the skittles first time. On her second go, she knocked down two.

'High scoring game!' joked Peter. 'Who's next?'

'When's your birthday, Sam?' Frankie asked him.

'November the twenty-sixth,' said Sam.

'What an incredible coincidence!' said Frankie. 'Mine's the twenty-seventh! I'm one day younger than you, so I go first.'

Oh, terrific!

'Actually, it's a proven statistic that in any group of eight people, there'll usually be two people with exactly the same birthday, so it's not that much of a coincidence,' I told them sourly. They just ignored me.

Frankie took her run up with the ball. She sent it really hard and it knocked down eight of the skittles. When she turned round she looked a bit embarrassed because she'd done so well.

'Yesss!' said Sam, punching the air. 'Wow! I thought *I* was good at it . . .'

Why didn't he just put a sock in it?

'Who's older out of you two?' asked Charlie, looking at me and Daisy. Daisy lifted her shoulders and buried her head again as though she was too shy to say her age. I felt as though I was years older than her. It was quite insulting to think she was thirteen.

'My birthday's in February,' I said a bit

snappily. I didn't want to say the exact date because people always made jokes about it.

'So is mine!' said Daisy, her head poking right out of its shell and a big grin appearing on her shiny face. 'What date's yours?'

'Fourteenth,' I mumbled.

'Oh, mine's the twenty-third.'

'You go next then.'

'The postman thinks Ollie's really popular when he delivers all these cards on Valentine's Day,' Sam told Frankie with a grin.

Frankie giggled. I ignored her and watched Daisy. She had the wrong foot in front, she didn't bend down properly, she didn't follow through and the ball trickled along as though it was entering the slowest ball of the year competition. By a miracle it clipped one of the skittles.

'One better than me,' said Charlie, smiling at Daisy. 'I think it's going to be up to Ollie and

Sue to get the points for our team.'

Daisy's second go was exactly the same as her first.

'At least you're consistent,' said Peter.

'Right, my go,' said Sam, picking up one of the really heavy balls.

'Whoa! A professional!' Peter said, eyeing the ball.

Sam grinned and took his throw. It went straight down the middle and knocked over every single skittle.

'Strike!' said Frankie, jumping up and down. 'You're really great at it, Sam!'

Sam was wearing this over-the-top cool expression that he'd probably been practising in front of the mirror. I felt the approach of another severe attack of chucking up.

'Your go, Ollie,' said Charlie.

My heart was beating fast. I'd feel so stupid if I didn't knock at least six down. I decided to take a heavy ball like Sam's, because it looked like they were the best. I threw the ball as hard as I could, which hurt my hand, but at least it rolled fast. It was pretty straight too. Seven skittles went down. Mum clapped and Daisy said, 'Good one, Ollie!'

I didn't look at anyone, just took my other shot and prayed. The remaining three skittles were all knocked down.

'Half strike! That's great, Ollie,' said Charlie. 'Our team stands a chance, after all.'

Mum and Peter both scored eleven, so the game was looking pretty even. And that's the way it carried on. Except that Sam went from strength to strength. How could he be so good at bowling when he was useless at every other sport? The trouble was, he *knew* he was impressing everyone and it made him even more cocky. He was hardly recognisable as Sam Cotteril. He was acting more like Robbie

Williams. And it was pretty obvious it was all for Frankie's benefit.

There was only one thing for it. I'd have to have a word with the Almighty. I'd never believed in proper praying before, but I was feeling desperate, and if I had to watch Frankie smiling and jumping up and down one more time because Sam had played yet another good shot, I'd go round the twist.

I made it look like I was studying the scores on the computer screen, but really I was saying this prayer:

Dear God, I know you're probably busy, but if you could possibly take a glance at Brinton Bowlplex I'd be really grateful. You'll notice that there's a boy in lane 4 who needs some help to stop him being so vain. Could you please arrange it for him to throw the next few balls so badly that he doesn't knock a single skittle down? This will make him much more . . . kind of humble, you know. Sorry I haven't been all that good at praying until now, but I promise I'll pray twice a day for ever if you could do this for me. Thank you very much. Amen.

Then I waited. Apart from Rory, Daisy was the only one whose game improved. She'd started off looking and playing like a giant tortoise, but after five or six goes she was almost as good as Sam. Peter had spent ages trying to help her to stand properly and showing her how to follow through, and it had paid off.

I was gobsmacked when she got her first strike.

'Wicked, Daisy!'

'Hey thanks, Ollie!' she said – practically the first words she'd spoken to me.

And as I looked at her gooey face two things happened. One: I had a brilliant brainwave, and two: I realised that it's true what people say.

God *does* move in mysterious ways. He must have decided that it would be a bit heavy to blatantly cock up Sam's game, so he'd come up with the cunning idea of me giving Daisy loads of compliments and attention, to make Frankie jealous. Then *she'd* stop drooling all over Sam, and *that* would wipe the stupid grin off Sam's face. Sorted! I only just stopped myself from laughing out loud.

I waited till Daisy had had her next go and scored a half strike, then said 'Yessss!' as I punched the air, just like Sam had done. 'Well done, Daisy. I can't believe you never played before today!'

She went bright pink.

'Really? You're not just saying it, are you?'

Out of the corner of my eye I could see Frankie watching me, so I decided I'd pull out all the stops.

'Course not. You're really brilliant.'

When I looked back on the whole afternoon I realised that what I'd said was bad enough, but what I did next was a hundred times worse. But once I'd done it, I could hardly take it back. I just had to put up with the sound of my immature little brother's voice whispering to Charlie, 'Did you see that? Ollie winked at Daisy!'

Why didn't he go and play on the motorway?

11 TORTURE (CONTINUED)

After the so-embarrassing wink (oh, why did I go that far?) Daisy wouldn't leave me alone. I know I wanted her to think I fancied her, but this was ridiculous! I should have stuck to giving her compliments. As if that wasn't bad enough, every so often Rory'd thrust his stupid grinning face right in front of mine and give me a big wink. I wanted to yell at him but I knew that would only make him do it more, so I had to ignore him, which took a whole lot of self-control, I can tell you.

The first game went on for ages and ages, and in the end Sam's team won. Daisy came and tucked her arm through mine and whispered, 'We'll win the next game – just you see!'

I prayed that someone might suggest we change teams, but no such luck. Daisy carried on playing really well. My play was no better and no worse, but Charlie and Mum got loads of strikes, and in the end our team won.

'You don't deserve to be on the losing side, Sam,' said Frankie. 'You're easily the best player here.'

'And Daisy's the most improved player,' I added, which made Daisy go all pink and silly.

We'd only booked two games so we went to the café afterwards.

'D'you fancy a game of air hockey, Ollie?' asked Sam.

Surprise, surprise. He's actually asking me, not Frankie. Wonders will never cease.

We went over to the air hockey table and I was about to put fifty pence in the slot when Sam grabbed my sleeve and came grinning up really close to me.

'She's brilliant, isn't she?' he said, jerking his head very unsubtly in Frankie's direction. 'It's incredible. I've never fancied anyone before, and I think she actually fancies me too. She keeps smiling at me.'

'No, she acts like that with everyone. She would have told me if she fancied you. She tells me everything, you see.'

I thought that might take the wind out of his sails, but it was like I hadn't even spoken.

'You're lucky having her as a sister, but on the other hand, I'm glad she's not *my* sister, because then I wouldn't be able to fancy her, would I? I can't wait till I can officially say she's my girlfriend, but first something's got to happen. And it's going to happen tomorrow.'

The more he talked, the more I wanted to hit him. The knot was tightening inside my stomach.

'She's not my sister, actually.'

'Yeah, but she *is* in a way, isn't she?'

'No, she's not in any way at all. We haven't got the same mother or the same father.'

'Yeah, but your mum's living with her dad, so she's your stepsister, right?'

'That's just a name.'

Sam must have got fed up with my arguments, because he quickly changed the subject. 'Do you like Daisy?'

'She's OK.'

'You're acting like she's fantastic!'

'I was just trying to be nice. She seemed a bit shy.'

'Well, she's not shy any more. Look. She's watching you right now.'

'Let's just play a game, shall we?'

'Don't you want to know what's going to happen tomorrow?'

'Not particularly.'

Not for a million pounds.

'I'm going to get Frankie to kiss me.'

That did it. I rammed the fifty pence piece into the slot and hit the disc so hard that it banged into the sides four times and finished up nearer me than Sam. Sam was getting far too up himself for my liking. How did he know we were even going to meet up again tomorrow? His eyes goggled behind his glasses as I whacked disc after disc into the sides at about eighty miles per hour and won the game fourteen-nil in two minutes flat.

I wondered if he was planning on taking those glasses off when he kissed Frankie. What a thought! I had to shake it out of my head before it took root. Unfortunately I was too late, because it came back to me about three times a minute, gutting me every time.

Frankie and Daisy came over when we finished our game.

'It'd be great if we could get together again tomorrow,' said Daisy. 'It's so boring with Mum and Pammy, isn't it, Sam?'

'My mum's made other arrangements for tomorrow,' I said.

'Like what?' asked Frankie.

'If it's fine, we're going to the beach,' I told her.

'What if it's not fine?' asked Daisy.

'We're going out for the day,' I answered.

Mum hadn't said a word about what we were going to do the next day, but nobody needed to know that.

'Do you think they'd mind if we came along too?' asked Daisy.

If my body had been a balloon, that remark would have made all the air go out of me. I couldn't be bothered to reply. I just wandered back to the others so I didn't hear how Frankie answered. One thing was certain though. No way was I going to spend another day with Sam and Daisy. It was too much effort pretending that I thought Daisy was a Britney Spears lookalike. There was no point anyway – Frankie obviously liked Sam better than me. All I could do was try and make sure we didn't see him and Daisy any more this holiday. At least then I'd get Frankie back to myself, even if she didn't actually like me as much as him.

'Can Daisy and Sam come with us to the beach tomorrow?' Charlie asked Mum a bit later.

'Well, that's up to Pammy, and Daisy's mum. It's fine as far as I'm concerned. Is that where you want to go then, the beach?'

'I thought that was what you'd arranged.'

Uh-oh! Diversion tactics needed.

'Oh look! There's your mum now, Sam!'

Everyone turned towards the door with welcoming smiles on their faces, and then all the smiles turned to looks of puzzlement as one by one they all turned back to me.

'Where?'

'Oh, sorry, I thought it was that woman there . . .'

'So you think my mum looks like *her*?' said Sam, grinning. 'I must tell Mum when she arrives. She'll be really flattered to know that Ollie got her mixed up with a tall, slim black woman carrying a baby.'

Daisy's face was one big frown. I knew what she was doing. She was wildly searching her mind for something to say to make me look less of a dipstick. I wished she wouldn't bother.

'I can see what Ollie means. It's that orange turban thing on her head, because your mum *does* wear a lot of orange, doesn't she, Sam?'

Of course everyone cracked up when she said that. Rory gave me another of his unsubtle winks then spoke to me behind his hand – the sickening little maggot.

'See your *girlfriend's* sticking up for you, Ollie. Pity Sam's after your other girlfriend, isn't it?'

'I couldn't care less,' I said.

'You *could* care less,' went on the ruthless turd. 'It's obvious you're jealous. That's the only reason you're being nice to Daisy.'

He'd only got it sickeningly right again, hadn't he? Was the kid psychic or something?

'Don't talk rubbish!'

Suddenly everyone was standing up. While Rory had been giving me severe earache, neither of us had noticed that Mrs C and Daisy's mum really had arrived. I expect everyone else in the place had noticed though, because they were sailing towards us, arms flying everywhere, big voices booming about the 'magnificent' concert.

'My dears, it was super! Absolutely *sooooooooper*! You really should have been there,' began Daisy's mum.

We went through the exit turnstiles to join them in the foyer.

'Oh, to sit in that audience, knowing that we had connections with the conductor, was just heavenly!' added Sam's mum, which was a weird thing to say, because she was about as connected to that conductor as I was to the Pope.

'Can Sam and I spend tomorrow with Ollie and everyone, Mummy?' asked Daisy.

My whole body groaned. If only I could rewind and start again from before that stupid wink!

'We'd love to have them,' smiled Mum.

'Well, if you're sure it's not too much trouble . . .' said Mrs Cotteril, giving her sister a sidelong look, which meant *Great! Looks like we can have some more sooooooper fun without the children, darling!*

'Well, that's settled,' said Mum. 'We're going to the beach as long as it's not pouring with rain or blowing a gale. So they'll need swimming things.'

'Would it be easiest if we drop Sam and Daisy at your holiday home?'

'Why not just meet us on the beach?' said Peter. 'I've heard two or three people saying it's going to be lovely and hot again tomorrow.'

'Good idea,' said Mum. Then she went to great lengths to explain exactly which bit of which beach. 'It might be an idea to exchange phone numbers. We'll take our mobile with us.'

'*Soooper!*' said Pammy as she scribbled on a bit of paper and handed it to Mum. 'What time will you be there?'

'By ten, so let's say any time after that.'

Then next thing I knew, Daisy's hot breath was right inside my earhole.

'One minute past, then!'

I forced myself to grin at her incredible wit, then wiped my ear as soon as they were all safely out of view.

Little did she know that plan B was about to be put into action.

12 THE NIGHTMARE BEGINS

At seven o'clock the following morning I was crouching behind the hedge on the other side of the road from our house, Mum's mobile in my hand and the bit of paper with Sam's aunt's number on it in my pocket. I'd been dreading not waking up early enough, but I needn't have worried. I'd woken up at six-thirty. Mum and Peter normally got up much later than that, so at least I wouldn't get caught in the act. I was as nervous as hell, but it had to be done.

I knew it was rather early to be phoning, but

it was vital that the whole thing sounded as realistic as possible and I reckoned Mum would have given Mrs C and her sister plenty of notice about our arrangements being altered. I got out the piece of paper that I'd nicked from Mum's bag last night, and punched in the number with shaky fingers. After a few seconds it started ringing, then my legs started shaking too, probably because I was crouching, but I couldn't stand up in case my head showed over the hedge. I covered the mouthpiece and practised Mum's voice for the fiftieth time.

After eight rings the answerphone message came on. At least I thought it was the answerphone. It was hard to tell because the voice kept on cutting out. I'd never thought of this happening and I began to panic a bit. I was about to disconnect, when Daisy's mum came on the line.

'Hello.' She sounded as though she'd been asleep.

This was it!

'Hello, Letitia. It's Sue Cranshaw here.' I'd heard Mum say 'Bye, Letitia' yesterday so I knew they were on first name terms.

'Sorry . . . the line's breaking up. *Who* is it?'

Great! She couldn't hear my voice properly. Less chance of getting sussed.

'I'm so sorry to disturb you at this ungodly hour –' (I liked that bit) – 'but I'm afraid Rory and Frankie are unwell, so we'll have to cancel today's arrangements.'

The effort of trying to make my voice sound like Mum's was making me sweat. Also, the tremble in my legs seemed to have spread to my voice.

'Oh Sue . . . Sorry, the line's very bad . . . Rory and Frankie what?'

'They're not well.'

'Oh, what a bore!'

'I'm going to have to cancel today.'

'Sorry, I missed that completely. Say again . . .'

'I'm going to have to cancel today,' I tried not to shout.

'Cancel? Oh, what an awful bore for you. Is it runny tummy? That's what Daisy had, you know.'

Daisy! Of course! I never thought of that. 'I think they probably caught it off Daisy.'

'I can hardly hear you, Sue, so I'll say bye bye now. Do give everyone our love. Hope they're better soon.'

'Yes. Bye.'

I didn't even wait for her answer, just disconnected and felt like dancing round the field, I was so happy. We wouldn't be bothered by Kissing Sam and his hot-breathed cousin any more! All I had to do was smuggle the phone back in before Mum noticed it was missing – which ought to be a piece of cake – and then act as surprised as everyone else when Sam and Daisy didn't show up.

'Coming, Frankie?' I asked.

It was just like it used to be. Charlie and Rory were already digging away, talking about making the biggest moat ever, because there were so few people on the beach, as we'd got there quite early. Mum was lying on her stomach and Peter was rubbing cream into her back. Frankie was scrunching her hair up and I was clutching both the body boards.

'Here, let me take one of them.'

As we were running down to the sea, which was quite far out again, I felt full of hope that today would be the day that would make everything go back to normal. We were just getting into the sea, when Frankie spoilt my lovely feeling by mentioning Sam.

'Is Sam as good at swimming as he is at bowling?'

I tried not to let it show, but she'd really rattled my cage. You see, if she was *talking* about Sam, then she must have been *thinking* about him.

'Nah. Useless. He hates getting wet. He can't even swim.'

That wasn't strictly true. Sam *had* learnt to swim but only just. I didn't think he'd want to do more than paddle in the sea. Whenever we had swimming at school last year he always stayed at the shallow end. He could swim widths, but he'd never dare attempt a length because that would mean going up to the deep end.

Frankie looked sympathetic.

'Poor old Sam. What about Daisy?'

'I've no idea – oh, wait a minute, she did say something about winning a diving competition.'

Frankie didn't make any comment. It was

obvious she didn't believe me. I don't know why I said it really. We were well into the sea by then and a big wave was coming up behind us.

'Race you!' I said.

It was a close one. She won by about half a metre.

'Not lost my touch!' she grinned, and that other horrible conversation seemed to vanish.

For about forty minutes we had brilliant fun. And then:

'It's weird that they haven't shown up yet, isn't it?' said Frankie.

'I bet their mothers take ages and ages getting ready to go out.'

'Oh no! My scrunchie's come off. My hair's getting sopping wet.'

'It can't have gone far,' I said, diving under to have a look. I was forgetting I wasn't in a swimming pool. My eyes were really stinging when I came up.

'I shouldn't have done that,' I said, rubbing them.

'Don't rub them, Ollie, you'll only make it worse. I'm just going back up to the others. I think Charlie's got a spare scrunchie.'

She went rushing off and I stood there blinking to try and get the salt out of my eyes. If only I had some ordinary cold water and then I could wash my face. I was on the point of going back to Mum for a towel when a horrible sight met my eyes.

At the back of the beach was an expanse of huge rocks, and beyond that was the road. There were walkways every so often between the rocks so that people could get from the road to the beach. From where I was in the sea it was practically impossible to see anything beyond the beach. I could make out Mum and the others, but only because of our big blue and white parasol. The people coming down the walkways looked like the tiniest dots. But my stomach flipped over at the sight of two dots that were slightly larger than the rest. A pink one and a red one. Oh God!

They'd obviously decided to come anyway. And they'd only got to turn right at the bottom of that walkway and they'd be heading straight for our spot. The game would be up. My sins would find me out. Oh, what a mess! What a totally stupid mess!

But then a small miracle happened because they turned left. Maybe I wouldn't be sussed after all. As long as we didn't meet up in the sea, I reckoned we could avoid them on the beach. I couldn't imagine Mrs Cotteril or Daisy's mum wanting to go into the cold sea, and I bet Daisy wouldn't go in on her own. I'd just have to make sure nobody went on any long walks in their direction. The pink and red dots with the two smaller dots beside them were still walking along purposefully. The more they kept going, the better I felt.

Frankie was on her way back to the sea, her hair all scrunched up again. Just as she splashed her way up to me, the pink and red dots came to a standstill. Panic over. Frankie and I surfed for another few minutes, but I couldn't relax because I had to keep checking that the coast was clear.

'What are you staring at, Ollie?'

'The sky . . . up there. I was just thinking it's looking a bit overcast.'

She looked at me as though I was out of my mind. 'Ollie, it's bright blue!'

I was just wondering what to say to that, when she forgot all about the sky because her hair was flying loose.

'Oh no! Not again! I don't believe it! That's the second scrunchie I've lost. Charlie'll kill me.

Sorry, Ollie, I think I'll go and sunbathe for a bit.'

'Yeah, OK. I'll go for a walk. See you soon.'

I guessed Mum and Peter would be wondering what on earth had happened to Sam and Daisy. I didn't particularly want to be around for that conversation. I walked along at the edge of the sea for ages until I was way past the spot where Sam and the others were, then I went straight up the beach towards the road and nipped up one of the little walkways. Once on the road, I turned to go in the other direction and kept going until I reckoned I was directly above Sam and the others.

I trod gingerly on the rocks, keeping low and listening hard. Eventually I heard Daisy's mum talking. I stopped and crouched in a little dip in the rocks, a big boulder hiding me from anyone on the beach.

' . . . absolute bliss. I'm so glad we decided to

come anyway. Shopping with the children would have been a bit of a nightmare.'

They both chuckled. Then the next voice I heard was Sam's, only he sounded much louder. It took me a moment to work out that this was because he and Daisy must have been actually sitting on the rocks, only a couple of metres away from my boulder. They were to one side of me, and their mums were on the beach to the other side. So though I could hear both pairs talking, they couldn't hear each other.

'Oh, go *on*, Daisy,' Sam was saying. '*Pleeeease* come into the sea with me. This is so boring. I'd bet you'd go in if Ollie wanted you to.'

'Yes, I would. But he isn't here, is he?'

'Well, I'm not being boring just because Frankie's not here. Come on, Daisy. We can have one lilo each. You don't get cold or wet on a lilo.' I winced. Then I winced even more with his next words. 'I wonder if she's missing me. I bet she's really fed up, being ill.'

'Look, I'm trying to read this magazine, Sam. Can you be quiet, please?'

I'd heard enough and was about to go back to Frankie and the others when Mrs Cotteril's words stopped me.

'Well, would you believe it!'

My heart beat faster.

'Look over there, Letitia! Unless my eyes are deceiving me, that is Sue and Peter Cranshaw!'

My blood ran cold.

'My goodness, you're right. That's odd. Perhaps they decided the children were well enough after all.'

'You *are* sure you heard Sue right, Letitia?'

'Well . . . I'm beginning to wonder now. As I said, the line was terrible.'

'Look! The children are there! Well, bless me! They're playing away without a care in the world.'

'No, wait a minute. There are only three of them.'

My heart was banging against my ribs by this time. Their voices were getting louder, and I was afraid Sam and Daisy would hear them.

'It's Ollie who's missing. I wonder if Sue meant it was Ollie not Rory who was unwell. Maybe they decided he was old enough to be left alone for a little while.'

'Unless . . .' There was a long pause. 'No, it can't be . . .'

'What?'

'You don't think they were trying to get out of having Daisy and Sam with them?'

'No, no, no. I don't know Sue all that well, but I'm quite certain there's nothing artful about her. Let's pop over and have a word, shall we?' She lowered her voice and I only just caught what she said next. 'Better not tell Daisy and Sam at this stage.' Then she called out, 'We're just stretching our legs, you two. Back in a mo.'

I groaned. So this was it. The game was up.

13 SHOCK WAVES

Every muscle in my body tightened up. I didn't wait another second, just scrambled back up the rocks, ignoring the pain in the soles of my feet, ran for ages along the road, then went down a walkway on the other side of Mum and the others.

'Been running, Ollie? You're all puffed,' said Mum.

'I've just come from over there,' I said, pointing in the opposite direction to where Sam and Daisy were. 'It's really brilliant. There are rock pools and everything. Let's move places, shall we?'

'You're joking, Ollie. This is perfect,' said Mum in a lazy voice because she was half asleep in the sun.

'You've not said anything about our castle,' called Charlie. 'Look! Don't you think it's mega? We just need to fill up the moat now.'

I glanced along the beach. They were about a minute away. There was nothing I could do. I suddenly understood what it meant when people talked about 'burying your head in the sand'. Pity I couldn't bury my whole body.

'Oh, here they are at last,' said Frankie, sitting up. 'We thought you weren't coming!' she called out. 'Can you pass me my sun cream, Ollie? It's in that bag.'

'I'm going down to the sea.'

'Just pass Frankie her sun cream, Ollie,' said Mum.

'Hello,' said Peter to Mrs Cotteril and her

sister. 'Have you left your stuff in the car? Do you want a hand?'

Mum must have suddenly sensed that something was wrong.

'Where are Sam and Daisy, Pammy? Is everything all right?'

'I think that should be *our* question,' said Sam's mum, a bit snappily.

I was about to creep off when Frankie asked me to pass her sunglasses. I started rummaging in the bag that she was pointing at.

'Sorry?' said Mum, shielding her eyes from the sun and looking bewildered.

'I thought two of the children weren't well,' went on Mrs Cotteril.

'Sorry?' said Mum again, sounding puzzled.

'The last we heard, Frankie and Rory were unwell so this beach trip was off.'

'I don't understand. Who did you hear that from?'

'From you!'

'I'm afraid I'm really not following this.'

'Just tell us what on earth you're talking about,' said Peter, sounding a bit stroppy. I shot him a quick look. We all did. It was very rare for Peter to get riled by anything or anyone.

'At seven o'clock this morning we received a phone call from you, Sue, to say that Frankie and Rory were unwell so you were going to have to cancel today's arrangements.'

'But I . . . I . . .'

'Hold on a minute.'

That was Peter. He was scanning our faces. Mine, Frankie's, Charlie's and Rory's. He settled on mine.

'Do you know anything about this, Ollie?'

I had a split second to decide whether or not to come clean. And in that split second I heard Sam's smarmy voice in my mind . . . *I'm going to get her to kiss me.*

'No. Don't know what you're talking about.'

I managed to hold Peter's gaze until he moved on to Frankie. 'What about you?'

She shook her head and I saw suspicion in Peter's eyes.

He thinks it's her.

'Charlie? Rory? Anything to say before we pack up and go straight home?'

I'd never heard Peter sounding so angry before. Inside my head an argument raged.

Just own up.

I'll only get punished.

You deserve it.

But I might be able to get away with it.

The longer it goes on, the worse it'll get.

It can't be worse than having to put up with Sam and Daisy.

So you're prepared to ruin the rest of the holiday for everyone?

I can't own up now. Not in front of them all.

I'll do it as soon as I'm on my own with Mum or Peter.

Promise?

Promise.

'Well, Charlie?' Peter repeated.

'What exactly are you saying, Dad?' asked Charlie, standing up to her father in her usual way.

'I'm saying that Daisy's mum received a phone call this morning at seven o'clock and it was not made by Sue or me. So which one of you four is going to own up?'

'I didn't get up till a quarter to eight, so it wasn't me,' said Charlie. 'What time did you get up, Rory?'

Everyone knew that Rory was always first up. 'I don't know. I didn't even look at my watch, but Ollie wasn't in bed when I woke up.'

All eyes were back on me.

'Look, I've told you, it wasn't me . . .'

Mum suddenly took charge of the situation.

'Pammy, all I can do is to apologise profusely.'

'Don't worry, my dear. We're just along there. You can see our mauve parasol, can't you? It's the tall one.'

'Yes . . . thank you. Just give us a few minutes.'

There was a silence when they'd gone. Then Peter said, 'Right, I'm going to give you all one more chance to own up and if no one does, we go home. Simple as that.' There was another silence. 'And I mean *home*, not holiday house.'

He delivered this last stab in a low voice that made goosebumps come up on my arms even though the sun was shining. I glanced at Frankie. A tear was running down her face.

'I did it,' she said softly.

Charlie, Rory, Mum, Peter and I all stared at her, wide-eyed. I couldn't bear it any longer. Frankie must have been so desperate not to end the holiday she was prepared to take the blame for something that she hadn't even done.

'No, *I* did it,' I said. I looked Peter straight in the eye. 'I know I've done a terrible thing, but I just couldn't stomach the thought of those two being with us for yet another day. That's all. Sorry. You can punish me, Peter, but please don't make us all go home.'

Peter and Mum looked at each other, then Mum spoke to Charlie and Rory. 'Why don't you two go ahead and fill up your moat with water?'

Without a word they grabbed their buckets and went off. I was about to be blasted into oblivion. And yet when I looked back on this moment much later, all I could remember was the way Charlie and Rory had looked so odd, going down to the sea, their two thin tense bodies walking close together to try and ward off the awful atmosphere.

'I trust you're not just protecting Frankie, Oliver,' said Peter.

I think that was the first time he'd ever called me Oliver. It was like a double shock because I suddenly realised that he really didn't know which one of us had done it. Frankie stayed silent. I shook my head and looked down. When I looked back up again, he was peering into Frankie's face, as though to sniff out any lies that might be lurking inside her head.

There were lots of tears on her face, but she didn't make a sound when she was crying. I think I liked her more in that moment than I'd ever liked her before. She could have easily thrown a big wobbly and screamed at her dad that it wasn't her, but she didn't say a word.

I had to put her out of her agony.

'I got up really early and went outside with your mobile phone, Mum. I took it behind the hedge on the other side of the road and I imitated your voice and told Daisy's mum it was all off because of Frankie and Rory being ill.'

'But why, Oliver?' said Mum in a quiet voice. 'I mean, it's a bit drastic, isn't it? Why didn't you just tell me and Peter that you'd be happier if we didn't have Sam and Daisy for the day?'

'Because you'd think I was stupid and you'd tell the others and then Rory would take the mickey. And anyway, you wouldn't have been able to cancel it at such short notice.'

'Well, that's probably true, but at least we could have made sure we didn't make any further arrangements. We're all on this holiday together, Oliver. Everyone has a right to be happy.'

'Yeah, but I would have been outvoted. I knew I was the only one who didn't want them around.'

'You weren't, actually.'

Frankie had finally spoken. I couldn't believe my ears. I wanted to know what she meant, but Rory was racing back from the sea, shouting something and waving his arms frantically.

We strained to hear.

'Quick. Sam's fallen off the lilo!'

I shot up and set off full pelt.

'Oliver! Come back here!' I heard Peter's angry voice. 'You're not getting off that lightly.'

'For goodness' sake. He's only fallen off the lilo,' shouted Mum crossly.

But I had recognised the panic in Rory's voice.

'Sam can't swim!' I heard Frankie tell them, then I was too far away to hear another word.

14 THE KISS

I ran and ran, the wind drumming in my ears, the roar of the sea making my legs go faster and faster. As I got nearer I could see the lilo, but no Sam.

Charlie was standing by the edge, ready to direct me.

'Over there!' she screamed, pointing to the lilo.

'Tell Mum to phone for an ambulance or something,' I called over my shoulder as I kicked my way as far as I could into the sea, then plunged into the fastest crawl stroke I could manage, swimming hard till I knew I must be out of my depth. I was getting nearer and nearer to the lilo, yet Sam was nowhere to be seen. I dived under, keeping my eyes open. The sea stung my already sore eyes but I didn't care. Sam was under the lilo. His face looked strange. I grabbed hold of him under the arms and pushed him up to the surface, then realised that his weight was making us both go under. I had to get him on the lilo.

'Sam!' I said breathlessly. 'Can you hear me?'

His eyes were closed and his head was lolling. I was terrified. What if . . . I couldn't bear it if . . .

He was too heavy to put on the lilo. I knew then that I hadn't time to do anything other than struggle to the shore as best I could. I'd practised lifesaving lots of times in school swimming lessons, but this wasn't the same as trying it out on a partner who floated obediently on the surface, hanging lightly on to you, while you swam easily to the side. I used all my strength to try to keep Sam's head above water as I struggled along.

You could hardly call it swimming, what I did. I was kicking my legs violently and shoving the sea with my shoulders and head. I swallowed loads of water along the way and thought I was going to be sick. I could hear lots of people having fun swimming and splashing near by, but they didn't notice me in my little terrifying world, and I couldn't shout for help because I needed all my energy to stop Sam from going under. I felt sick and I thought my arms were going to drop off.

'Please don't die, Sam,' I spluttered, though I knew he couldn't hear me. 'You can kiss Frankie as much as you want. Just please don't die.'

And suddenly my feet were touching the

bottom and I could stand – except that I couldn't because my knees were crumbling. Someone was yelling and running towards me. It was Peter.

'Hang in there, Ollie. You've done brilliantly.'

He was really panting as I dropped Sam into his arms. Another man was instantly at our side. Between them they carried Sam on to the shore.

'I think he's going to need mouth to mouth,' the man said to Peter. 'I'm not too sure . . .'

'Er . . . neither am I. You're supposed to clear the airways first, aren't you?' said Peter. I saw that he was shaking.

'I'll do it,' I said, kneeling over Sam and taking charge.

This bit, I could remember well. Peter got out of the way quickly. I put two fingers under Sam's chin and tipped his head back.

Right, what's next? Check breathing. Look, listen, feel. Count to ten. Not breathing. OK, block

nose . . . mouth to mouth. Five breaths. Keep calm,
Ollie.

A small crowd was gathering. I was vaguely aware of toes clenching the sand near Sam's head. Nothing else.

Take pulse at Adam's apple. Yes! A pulse! But he was still unconscious. *What now? Keep doing it. Twenty breaths, check pulse, twenty breaths, take pulse . . . until help arrives.*

'You're doing well, Ollie,' said Peter, his voice still shaking.

Sam's mum had arrived on the scene. I could hear her wailing.

'I had no idea he'd gone into the sea.'

Mum and Daisy's mum were trying to calm her, but they didn't sound calm themselves.

'Don't worry, Pammy. He'll be all right.'

There were other voices too, but they were a blur. My head was swimming. I thought I couldn't last much longer. After every breath I gave Sam, I said *Please live* inside my head.

'The ambulance is on its way.'

The pulse was still there. Was it my imagination or was it weaker? If anything happened to Sam, it would be my fault. I'd never be able to bear it. Nothing mattered any more, except getting my friend back. *Surely someone will be here in a minute.*

And just at that very moment Sam threw up a load of sea water, then his chest shuddered. I sat back in a crouched position as he rolled over on to his side and opened his eyes.

'Oh Sam!' cried his mother, dropping on to her knees beside him.

As the ambulance men arrived with the stretcher, I stood up shakily.

'Someone's done a great job here,' said one of the men.

'It was my brother,' said Rory. 'His name's Ollie.'

Rory had tears in his eyes and was really shouting at the men as though they were deaf.

'Well, that's one brilliant brother you've got there, mate,' said the ambulance man as he helped the other man roll Sam on to the stretcher.

'He's *my* brother too!' came another voice. It was Frankie. She was suddenly beside me giving me an enormous hug. I couldn't hug her back because I still felt too weak.

'And mine!' Charlie called.

'Sounds like you've got a good bunch of brothers and sisters!' said the ambulance man to me.

Sam was trying to sit up. He looked totally confused and his eyes didn't seem to be focusing properly.

'All right, son, what's your name?'

'Sam,' he whispered.

'I'm his mother,' said Mrs Cotteril.

'We'll get Sam to hospital and check him over,' said the first ambulance man. 'Don't you worry now, my dear . . .' Then the man turned to me. 'What exactly happened, Ollie?'

'He saved Sam's life,' said Mrs Cotteril, bursting into tears as we all set off.

Peter's arm was round my shoulder and we both had shaky legs as we walked a few paces behind the stretcher. Mum was beside me on the other side.

'I'm so proud of you,' she whispered.

The three girls were walking behind with Daisy's mum but Rory was walking beside Sam, telling him all that had happened in a very loud slow voice, as though the sea might have addled Sam's brain.

'Ollie!' he suddenly called back to me. 'Sam wants you.'

I broke free from Peter and caught up with the stretcher. Sam looked up at me. I was glad to see his eyes were back to normal. In fact his whole face was back to normal, except he looked funny without his glasses.

'Thanks for saving my life, Ollie.'

I didn't know what to say. I couldn't really say, 'Oh, that's OK,' as though I'd lent him fifty pence or something.

'Ollie . . .'

He was beckoning me to bend down, so I did, rather awkwardly as I kept walking.

'I knew I'd get to kiss *someone* today. I just never guessed it'd be you!'

An hour before I would have happily throttled him for a remark like that. But now, for some unknown reason, I didn't care. I really didn't care.

15 FRIENDS

It was six o'clock in the evening and Frankie and I were sitting side by side on a wall in the garden. All the others were inside the house setting up the score sheet for another tournament.

'Sorry about today,' I said without looking at her.

'You've already said sorry, Ollie. You don't need to keep saying it.'

'I know I've apologised to Mum and Peter, but I haven't apologised to you. And I haven't said thanks either.'

'What for?'

'Taking the blame so we wouldn't have to go home early.'

'It was the only way I could thing of getting you to own up.'

'What do you mean?'

'Well, I know my dad. And today it was pretty obvious that unless one of us owned up, we were in for some kind of awful punishment. I knew you were too nice to let me take the blame . . .'

She smiled at me. It was one of those really genuine smiles that I'd seen her giving Sam. This time yesterday, I was a stupid lovesick teenager and that smile would have sent me up to forty-seventh heaven. But today everything was different. It was impossible to explain – even to myself – what had changed. It was when I was struggling through the sea desperately trying to save Sam, that I'd suddenly realised friendship was the most important thing. The only thing that counted. All I wanted now was to have Frankie as my best friend. I knew it would take time, though.

She was biting her lip, watching me biting *my* lip. There was so much I wanted to talk to her about, but I didn't want to say anything that would make her think I was a complete dork.

'When we were on the beach, you told Mum and Peter that I wasn't the only one who didn't want Sam and Daisy to join us today.'

'Yeah. That was true.'

'Why?'

'You'll think I'm horrible.'

'I won't. Honest.'

She looked down and mumbled, 'I thought you fancied Daisy and I didn't want my brother going out with someone as uncool as her.'

'Oh . . . er . . . yeah . . .' She'd really surprised me. 'Sorry about that,' I said, feeling embarrassed about the way the conversation was going.

'Please tell me you don't fancy her.'

'No, I don't. You see, I thought you fancied Sam, and –'

'Fancied Sam? You've got to be joking! What ever made you think that?'

I suddenly felt stupid. 'Well, you seemed to be kind of talking to him and stuff . . .'

'Talking to him? Since when did talking to someone mean you fancy them? I was just being friendly.'

Then I *really* felt stupid. 'Well, he fancies you,' I mumbled.

'Yeah, I worked that one out. That was the other reason I didn't want those two around for another day. It was easy being friendly for one afternoon, but when Daisy wanted them both to join us *again* I felt suicidal. And there's another thing . . .'

'What?'

'You'll think I'm stupid.'

For the second time I assured her I wouldn't.

'Well, you see those first few days on the beach were so fantastic, and then everything seemed to go wrong. You didn't seem to like me much any more . . .'

'Yeah, I did. It's just that Rory – well, Rory gets things wrong a lot . . . and he might have thought I fancied you, or something totally stupid like that. So I didn't want to seem too . . . you know . . . friendly.'

She looked at me carefully and I knew I was going red, but there was nothing I could do about it.

'I wish I'd known that. You see, I'd been so happy to find that I got on absolutely brilliantly with my brother, and I just wanted those first few days to go on for ever. Then I heard you telling Rory that if you were dreaming about me, it must have been a nightmare, and I thought you didn't like me after all.'

I felt terrible when she said that. 'It was just to shut Rory up. Honest.'

'I believe you now. The trouble is, once we're all back home again, I won't get to see you very much, but you can see Sam whenever you like. And then there was Daisy. It was jealousy, I suppose. I didn't want those two around because I wanted you all to myself. Simple as that.'

Suddenly everything was clear. Frankie didn't fancy me *or* Sam, and she never had done. She just liked me as a brother and wanted me to like her as a sister. I felt really happy all of a sudden. Maybe one day she'd even want me as her best friend.

'Come on!' Mum called out to us. 'We're

about to start the tournament. You two are partners.'

'And guess what?' said Rory as we went in to join the others.

'What?'

'Peter's going to ask Charlie's mum if Charlie can come over more often from now on.'

Frankie and I looked at each other and slowly broke into big smiles. It was such an obvious solution.

'What are you two grinning about?' asked Rory.

'You,' I told him. 'We're thinking what a clever thing you've just said.'

Rory looked at us suspiciously.

'No, really,' said Frankie. 'It's the best thing that's happened this whole holiday. Apart from Ollie saving the life of his second best friend in the world,' she added.

'Second best? So who's his *best* friend then?'

asked Rory, looking as puzzled as I felt.

'Me, of course,' she told him. Then she turned to me and smiled.

So when Rory gave me yet another of his big slow-motion winks, it didn't wind me up one little bit. In fact I just cracked up laughing! And so did Frankie.

What happens next in the step-chain?

Meet Lissie in

SHE'S NO ANGEL

1 THE BOMBSHELL

'Hiya, folks!' said Leanne, chucking her school bag on her desk, which was just across the aisle from mine.

Her three good friends gathered round immediately.

'What have you been up to this weekend, Leanne? You've got that look on your face again!'

Leanne giggled.

I dread this time, first thing Monday morning, when you talk about what you've been doing at the weekend. Today I'd happened to come in at exactly the same time as Leanne, so all the attention would be on her. She's the sort of leader of the group, whereas I'm only on the edge because I'm not as good at making friends. Everyone always gathers round Leanne, and right now she was looking as though she was about to report something really interesting. With any luck I might escape the Monday morning interrogation.

'I went to London!' She announced, looking round proudly.

Gasps went up.

'How come you never told us on Friday?' asked Donna.

Leanne suddenly let out her breath and pulled a face as she spoke slowly. 'Because it was nothing great. It was my brother's graduation ceremony, and though Mum and Dad were in seventh heaven for the entire weekend, I was actually so bored I counted the bricks in the wall behind the stage!'

Everyone laughed. Leanne always makes people want to talk to her and laugh with her. I wish I could do that. Even when she's had a boring weekend, she's still swinging along happily.

'I went to my cousin's birthday party on Saturday night and it was fantastic!' said Donna.

'You lucky thing!' said Leanne, pouting and pretending she was jealous.

'I danced for three solid hours! The music was brilliant!'

'Yeah, and Donna and I went shopping in that new precinct,' said Jo. 'Mum was in a really good mood. She gave me an advance on my allowance and I bought those black trousers I wanted *and* that pink top!'

I pretended to be looking in my school bag, and started silently chanting my usual prayer for every other Monday morning: *Please don't ask me what I've been doing.* I can't bear it when they all look at me as though they feel sorry for me, so recently I've started pretending I've had a great time at my mum's. I'm not sure they're convinced though, and that makes it even worse. They probably talk about me afterwards behind my back.

'What did you do, Gemma?'

I breathed out. I was off the hook again.

'My aunt and uncle came for the weekend.'

'Cool! The uncle who works at Channel 4?'

'Yeah. He told us some great stories.'

I couldn't scrabble around in my bag for ever and as I glanced up I saw Leanne looking at me. Uh-oh! Here we go.

'What did *you* do, Lissie?'

I frowned at my nails then began to gnaw at one of them. I was getting very good at appearing unconcerned when inside I was completely churned up.

'Oh, nothing much . . .'

'Was it your weekend to go to your mum's?'

'Yeah.'

There was a pause and I could feel everyone's eyes on me. They were waiting for me to say something else. But how could I tell them what had really happened?

We went to Toby and Petronella's school fête on Saturday afternoon, where they both got to do and buy just about everything they wanted, and when they didn't win the games, they sulked. On Sunday morning I practised my cello which wasn't easy, because my half-sister was deliberately playing her music loudly in her bedroom.

I didn't say anything.

'What did you do on Saturday? Anything good?'

This was it. Either I had to tell the truth and admit that I'd had a totally terrible time because I couldn't stand my eight-year-old half-sister and my five-year-old half-brother, or I had to tell the usual lie and pretend that I'd had a great time. But I felt so pathetic admitting that I'd had another miserable weekend. It made me look stupid for not doing something about it. And I knew I *was* stupid. It was just so much easier to suffer in silence. After all, it was only two little days out of every fourteen – or even sometimes only one. And they *were* my half-sister and -brother.

'Nothing much . . .' I quickly changed the subject. 'Has anyone got any nail polish remover on them?'

I didn't miss the look that passed between Donna and Leanne. I bet they were thinking, *Fancy putting up with spending every other weekend with two children you can't stick. How sad is that?*

It was a quarter past six when Dad got home.

Gemma's mum had just dropped me back from music club, as she did every Monday.

'Hi, Liss,' Dad said to me, as he started opening the mail. 'How was school?'

'Fine.'

. I was sure he wasn't concentrating on me at all.

'We had choir practice at lunchtime.'

'Uh-huh.'

He screwed up the contents of the envelope, made a ball out of it and aimed it at the bin, before opening the next envelope.

'And I got C minus for that biology homework that you helped me with. So thanks very much, Dad.'

'Uh-huh.'

He was scanning through a phone bill, a frown on his face.

'We had some visitors at school this afternoon.'

'Uh-huh.'

Right, Dad, let's see if you're really listening.

'Yeah. Some gorillas. They just strolled in and started taking over from the teachers.'

'Uh-huh.'

'One of them was called Goliath, and I hope you don't mind but I liked him so much that I've signed the adoption papers and he's up in my bedroom watching television with a banana and a bag of cheese and onion crisps.'

Dad stopped reading and gave me a vague sort of smile. 'That's great,' he said. 'Sorry – who did you say was upstairs?'

'You weren't listening to a single word I said, Dad.'

'Yes I was!' he protested. 'I just didn't hear who you said was in your room.'

'Goliath the gorilla!' I informed him, with a withering look, to show him just how hopeless he was.

He looked a bit embarrassed then. 'Sorry,

Liss. Has my black shirt come out of the wash?'

'I think so. Why? Are you going out?'

'Yes, in about an hour. I'm going to . . .'

He broke off and sat down at the table. Suddenly I knew that he was about to say something important. Half a dozen possibilities flashed through my mind. Maybe he and Pauline had had a big row and Dad had found himself a new girlfriend. That would be terrible because I really like Pauline. Dad's only been going out with her for about a month, but he seems so happy. I'd hate it if they broke up. She isn't the first girlfriend Dad's had since he and Mum split up all those years ago, but even though I've only met her a few times I've got a feeling she's something special, and that Dad thinks so too.

Maybe he's taking her out for dinner and he's going to propose to her. That would be great! I'd get to be a bridesmaid. Then she could come and live in this house and I'd feel like I was in a proper family again. OK, I knew I was only building castles in the air, because you don't usually get married when you've only known someone a month.

Dad was looking at me carefully. 'The thing is, Liss . . . Pauline and I . . .' My heart hammered, ' . . . are going away together. Someone at work has got a place in Portugal, and we're going to rent it. So this evening we're meeting this chap and his wife to sort out the details.'

It was weird. It was like a bombshell without an explosion. I couldn't work out what the big deal was. It was great that Dad and Pauline had decided to have a holiday together. Maybe that would make them want to live together all the time. So why was my heart still banging away?

With Dad's next words I suddenly knew.

'You'll be staying at Mum's, Liss.'

He was giving me one of those encouraging

smiles that you give little kids when you're telling them how great it is at the dentist's.

I didn't want him to feel guilty about going away with Pauline, because Dad hardly ever does anything except work, so I tried to sound unfazed.

'How long for?'

Please let it only be a week.

'A fortnight.'

My heart stopped hammering and plummeted to my toes.

Collect the links in the step-chain . . .

1. To see her dad Sarah has to stay with the woman who wrecked her family. Will she do it? Find out in *One Mum Too Many*

3. Lissie's half-sister is a spoilt brat, but her mum thinks she's adorable. Can Lissie make her see what's really going on? Find out in *She's No Angel*

4. Becca's mum describes her boyfriend's daughter as perfect in every way. Can Becca bear to meet her? Find out in *Too Good To Be True*

5. Ed's stepsisters are getting seriously on his nerves. Should he go and live with his mum? Find out in *Get Me Out Of Here*

6. Hannah and Rachel are stepsisters. They're also best friends. What will happen to them if their parents split up? Find out in *Parents Behaving Badly*